**DARRELL PITT** began his lifelong appreciation of literature when he read the Sherlock Holmes stories as a child, quickly moving on to H.G. Wells and Jules Verne. This early reading led to a love of comics, science fiction and all things geeky. Darrell is now married with one daughter. He lives in Melbourne.

**Other books by Darrell Pitt**

*The Boy from Earth*

*A Toaster on Mars*

**THE JACK MASON ADVENTURES**

*Book I The Firebird Mystery*

*Book II The Secret Abyss*

*Book III The Broken Sun*

*Book IV The Monster Within*

*Book V The Lost Sword*

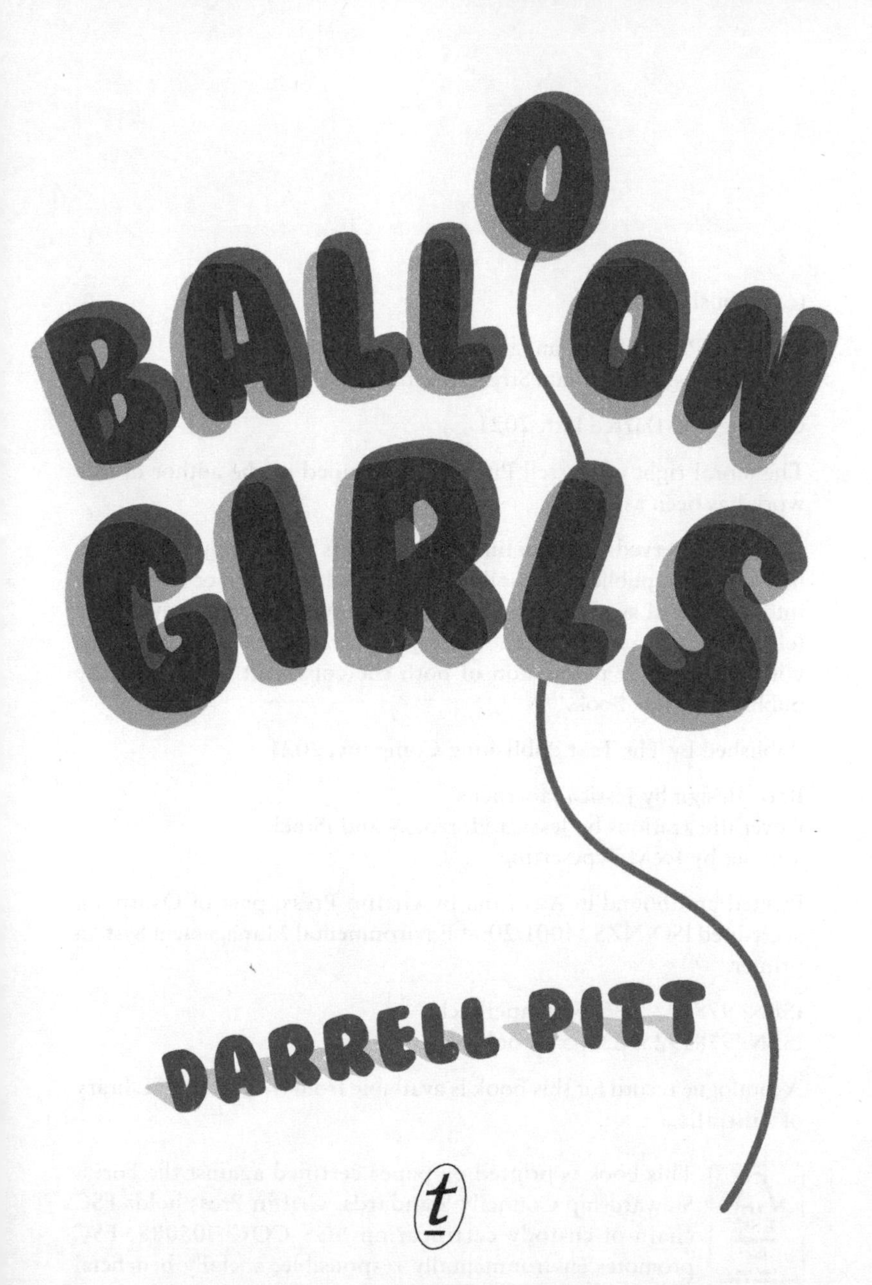


TEXT PUBLISHING MELBOURNE AUSTRALIA

textpublishing.com.au

The Text Publishing Company
Swann House, 22 William Street, Melbourne Victoria 3000, Australia



Published by The Text Publishing Company, 2021

Book design by Jessica Horrocks
Cover illustrations by Jessica Horrocks and iStock
Typeset by J&M Typesetting

Printed and bound in Australia by Griffin Press, part of Ovato, an accredited ISO/NZS 14001:2004 Environmental Management System printer.

ISBN: 9781922330567 (paperback)
ISBN: 9781925923865 (ebook)

A catalogue record for this book is available from the National Library of Australia.

This book is printed on paper certified against the Forest Stewardship Council® Standards. Griffin Press holds FSC chain-of-custody certification SGS-COC-005088. FSC promotes environmentally responsible, socially beneficial and economically viable management of the world's forests.

*Dedicated to the three most important women in my life: my wife, my daughter and my mum.*

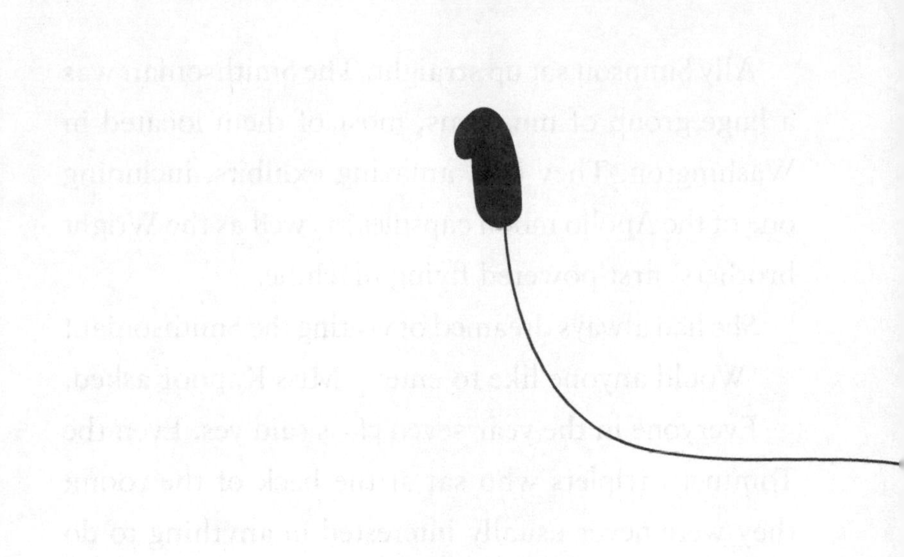

**'SOMETHING SPECIAL** is happening this term,' Miss Kapoor began. 'The Australian Scientific Education Association—ASEA—has announced a contest for year seven students.

'Working in teams of three, you must create a science project that shows your understanding of the scientific method. The team in first place will win a trophy—'

'Boring,' Bob Tommetti, a boy at the back of the classroom, muttered loudly enough for everyone to hear.

'—and an all-expenses-paid trip to the Smithsonian in the United States.'

Ally Simpson sat up straight. The Smithsonian was a huge group of museums, most of them located in Washington. They held amazing exhibits, including one of the Apollo moon capsules, as well as the Wright brothers' first powered flying machine.

She had always dreamed of visiting the Smithsonian!

'Would anyone like to enter?' Miss Kapoor asked.

Everyone in the year seven class said yes. Even the Tommetti triplets who sat at the back of the room; they were never usually interested in anything to do with school.

Miss Kapoor cast an approving eye over the group. 'I had no idea so many of you would be interested,' she said. 'I'll get some more application forms. In the meantime, take out your homework and turn to page sixty of the textbook.'

The moment Miss Kapoor left the classroom, a ball of paper bounced off the back of Ally's head.

'Get lost!' she snapped at the boys at the back of the room.

'What's wrong?' Bill Tommetti said. 'Didn't Weight Watchers work out?'

'What did you do?' Ben Tommetti chimed in. 'Fall in a pot of red paint?'

The Tommetti triplets were always giving Ally a hard time about her size—when they weren't making fun of her red hair.

'Drop dead!' said Harmony Smith, one of Ally's best friends. 'You guys are cavemen!'

'Yeah,' chimed in Ping Chong, Ally's other best friend. 'Cavemen!'

The boys' only response was to make *ugging* sounds.

'Ignore them,' Ping said from across the aisle as they took out their homework.

'I will,' Ally said. 'They're a medical miracle. They walk and talk—but they have no brains.'

'I should booby trap their seats with high explosives,' Harmony muttered. 'And then—*kaboom!*'

Harmony didn't live up to her name. Her mother, blonde-haired and calm, ran the local hippy bookshop, and was always advising people to be one with the universe. By comparison, Harmony was pale with long, black hair and black-rimmed glasses, and she was always planning violent revenge upon anyone who crossed her. Her favourite band, unsurprisingly, was a death metal band called Blood Guzzling Unicorns.

'The Tommetti triplets are evidence that Neanderthals are alive and well,' Ping agreed. 'Although they may not be Neanderthals. They could be Cro-Magnon. Or Australopithecus. Or—'

Some people had overactive imaginations. Ping had an overactive brain.

Miss Kapoor returned. She handed out the application forms as she collected the homework from last term. All the students handed in papers, but Ally noticed the papers from the Tommetti triplets looked very thin.

'Are you sure your project is five pages in length?' Miss Kapoor asked Ben.

He nodded vigorously. 'Sure is, miss,' he said.

Miss Kapoor peered at the pages. 'The printing is very big,' she said, frowning. 'And it's written in crayon?'

Ben nodded. 'I wanted it to be colourful,' he said.

Ally studied the application form. It had the ASEA logo in one corner, and the Smithsonian logo in the other.

The Smithsonian!

The teacher finished collecting the pages. Returning to the front, she put them down in a pile and turned to the class.

'Let's have a recap of the scientific method,' Miss Kapoor said. 'Can anyone tell me the five steps? Bob? How about you?'

Bob scratched his head. 'I remember we covered them,' he said. 'There are a couple I don't remember.'

'Which ones are they?'

'The first steps, the ones in the middle, and the last ones.'

'So...all of them.'

'Uh...yeah.'

Miss Kapoor turned to the class. 'Would anyone like to help Bob?' she asked.

The new boy, Jamie Trenthouse, put up his hand. He was tall and stick-skinny, and he had blazing red hair, like Ally. 'The first is to ask a question,' he said. 'You need to work out what you want to know.'

Miss Kapoor nodded. 'Can anyone think of an example of something we could investigate?' she asked.

Bruce Ricci, a quiet boy with black hair and dark eyes, raised his hand. 'Could we investigate Hicky Saw?' he asked.

Nobody said a word. Hicky Saw was the town legend. He supposedly haunted the streets of Yallaroo at night, armed with a saw, ready to cut off arms and legs without warning.

'All right,' Miss Kapoor said. 'We might ask this question: *Does the ghost of Hicky Saw haunt the town at night?* And what's the second step?'

'Gather information,' Ping said.

'Correct,' Miss Kapoor said. 'Which means we would search for photographic evidence that Hicky Saw is real—and not just a local legend. What's step three?'

Ally answered this one. 'You need to form a hypothesis,' she said.

'That's right,' Miss Kapoor said. 'A hypothesis is often written as an *if-then* statement. For example, *if* I clean my teeth, *then* I won't suffer from tooth decay.' She paused. 'In the case of Hicky Saw, a hypothesis we might formulate could be: If Hicky Saw exists, then we should be able to capture his image on video.'

Someone made a moaning sound and everyone laughed.

'Okay,' Miss Kapoor continued. 'What's the fourth step of the scientific method?'

Ally spoke up again. 'Do an experiment to test the

hypothesis,' she said. 'So we'd actually set up cameras to try and film Hicky Saw.'

'Correct,' Miss Kapoor said. 'And the fifth step?'

'Draw a conclusion,' a girl named Charlotte Bonnet said.

'Excellent!' Miss Kapoor said. 'You make a decision about whether your experiment confirmed what you thought or not.'

The lesson continued, but Ally was hardly able to focus. When the bell rang, she cornered Harmony and Ping in the hallway.

'Well?' she said.

'Well, what?' Harmony asked.

'The contest!'

'What about it?' Ping asked.

'We've got to enter the contest!' Ally said. 'And win!'

**ALLY SHUFFLED** her feet as she waited impatiently at the school bus stop. She felt like she was melting. The spring day had turned hot, and she and most of the Tamleigh High School kids were taking refuge under the huge ironbarks growing at the side of the road.

'It's boiling,' Harmony groaned.

'Is it?' Ally said. 'I hadn't noticed.'

'It must be over thirty degrees,' Ping said. 'Could even be thirty-five. Maybe even...'

A rattling sound came from around the corner and the Yallaroo school bus appeared. It swayed all over the road like a wombat with poor vision before its brakes screeched and it skidded to a halt.

The doors clattered open. 'Get on!' the driver rasped.

He was obviously having a bad day too.

The kids clambered aboard.

Harmony gave Ally a broad wink as the new boy, Jamie Trenthouse, took a seat near the front.

'What?' Ally said.

'You know what,' Harmony said.

'No, I don't know what.'

Harmony and Ping leaned in close.

'He *likes* you,' Harmony said.

'He does,' Ping agreed. 'I'm sure of it. Almost sure.'

'Don't be silly,' Ally said. 'Anyway, I'm focused on my mind. Not on being a kissy-kissy lovebird.'

'You two are ideally suited to each other,' Ping said. 'Apart from in the ways that you're not.'

'So much red hair,' Harmony said, shaking her head. 'You could cause a volcanic eruption. The whole town could melt into the Earth.'

'You two are ridiculous,' Ally groaned.

'We are,' Harmony agreed, 'but we're right.'

The school bus clattered away from the school and weaved through the town. Everything was dry and dust was everywhere: on houses, people and things. The whole region was in a drought and water restrictions were in place. People couldn't water their gardens or use a hose to clean their car.

*It's going to be a long, hot summer*, Ally thought.

The bus made its way out of town and down country roads, ejecting kids along the way until it finally reached Ally's home on the outskirts of Yallaroo. Her house was an old weatherboard building with a verandah that leaned terribly at one end and weeds clogging the front yard.

Adjacent to the building was her father's business, Simpson's Repair Yard, a tractor and farm equipment repair business. A high metal fence ran around the outside. Within lay a workshop, and the rusting bodies of dozens of tractors, harvesters, and other huge pieces of farming equipment that Russell had been unable to save.

Ally disembarked and made her way into the comparative coolness of her home. Her dachshund, Winston, came charging down the hall, and she gave him a big hug.

'Have you missed me?' Ally asked.

Winston barked in response.

Ally went to the kitchen and poured herself a glass of cold water from the fridge.

'Is that you, Ally?' her father called out.

'Who else would it be?'

'A criminal trying to steal our water?'

'It's not worth stealing,' Ally said, taking a sip.

She made her way to the lounge room where she found her dad standing before an easel with a brush in hand.

'What do you think?' Russell Simpson asked.

Her father's hobbies included stamp collecting and bird watching, but his chief interest was painting. His latest masterpiece was of an old man on the verandah of a house surrounded by bush, and it was almost completely identical to the other sixty-two paintings in Ally's home. Russell had learnt to paint from an online course, and it showed.

'That's a very interesting...tree,' Ally said, pointing.

'Thanks,' Russell said.

'It looks a lot like a person.'

'It *was* a person,' Russell confessed, 'but I decided to turn it into a tree.'

'Okay.' Ally considered this. 'And that *is* an old man on the verandah?'

'It is.'

Ally peered closer. 'He has three arms,' she said.

Russell stared at the picture. 'So he does,' he said. 'Well, that's easily solved.'

The oil painting was still wet. He used the sleeve of his overalls to smear the third arm into the background.

'There,' he said. 'Perfect!'

Ally didn't contradict him.

Her father had a red bushy beard, unruly dark hair, and wore grubby overalls. These same overalls doubled for when he was working on the engines of farm machinery, so they were smeared with both grease and paint.

As Russell rushed off to find a place where he could hang the picture, Ally wondered—yet again—how he could find the time to paint paintings, but not their own home.

The front doorbell jangled as he returned.

'I hope that's not Mrs Blunt complaining again,' Ally said.

Their neighbour was always complaining about something. They went down the hallway and glanced out the front window.

'Mmm,' Russell said. 'It *is* Mrs Blunt.'

'She's a *horrible* old woman,' Ally said.

Russell forced a smile. 'We must have a positive attitude,' he said, opening the door.

'Mrs Blunt!' Russell said.

'Mrs Blunt!' Ally echoed.

Winston growled at the old woman.

'Russell Simpson!' Mrs Blunt snapped. She was a thickset woman with grey hair in a bun, and a huge wart on her left cheek that danced when she spoke. 'I must complain about your dog!'

'Winston?' Russell said. 'What about him?'

'He was barking all night!'

'I'm sure he didn't make a sound.'

'He was barking! On and on and on!'

'Maybe you imagined it,' Ally said.

Mrs Blunt rolled her eyes. 'I'm not losing my mind, young lady,' she said, 'although sometimes I think I must be mad to stay in this town.'

Ally peered past her and down the street where two empty, rundown weatherboard homes lay. Beyond these were endless browning, ryegrass covered hills. Yallaroo had been hit particularly hard by the drought. Sheep farmers had gone broke. The local bank had closed. People had moved away.

Only the brave, foolish or—as Mrs Blunt had suggested—crazy, had stayed. Ally wondered which category she and her dad fitted into.

'You could move,' Russell pointed out.

'Over my dead body!' Mrs Blunt declared. Winston gave a hopeful bark, and she glared at him. 'My dear auntie Doris left me that home!'

Ally remembered Doris Blunt. She had been a friendly old lady, but Ally couldn't remember Mrs Blunt ever visiting her.

'Our town is going through a tough time,' Russell said.

'A tough time? This town is dying!'

'We need to have hope,' Ally said.

'Hope!' Mrs Blunt snorted.

'Hopes and dreams are what make life worth living,' Russell said.

'The only life around here is my lemon tree,' Mrs Blunt said, pointing proudly at the tree. 'It's the only thing around here that...that...*aaarrggh*!'

Winston had chosen that moment to wander into her yard and lift his leg against the tree.

'Winston!' Russell yelled. 'Come away from there!'

The dachshund trotted back over.

Ally tried not to laugh, but Mrs Blunt looked more furious than ever.

'No one in this dirty little town has ever achieved anything,' she said, 'and no one ever will!' She stormed off home.

'There's no pleasing some people,' Russell said.

But the old woman's words stayed with Ally. She couldn't get them out of her mind, even when she was trying to read in bed that night. The book she was reading was about Stephen Hawking, one of the greatest scientists of all time. Ally had a picture of him in his wheelchair on the wall above her desk. When she sat there, working on her homework, she looked up at him sometimes and felt encouraged, as though his lopsided smile was aimed right at her.

Ally closed the book carefully.

Above her bed was a huge poster of the moon. On the wall opposite was another, of the Andromeda galaxy. Under it were pictures of scientists Albert Einstein and Alexander Graham Bell. Stuck on the side of her bookcase was a photo of pioneering aviator Amelia Earhart and on the ceiling was a picture of NASA mathematician Katherine Johnson.

Posted on the wall directly over her desk was a picture of Marie Curie, the first woman to win a Nobel Prize. There was a book at the library about her that Ally had read at least five times.

A gentle knock came at her door.

'Come in.'

'Ready for bed?' her father asked.

'Dad,' Ally said, 'is Mrs Blunt right?'

'About what?'

'That no one in this town has ever done anything.'

'People do things all the time.'

'I mean…done anything amazing.'

Russell frowned. 'Well,' he said, 'there was that boy who made it into the second grade rugby team. And there was a girl who was in that tap dancing world record attempt, and the woman who…'

By the time he finished, Ally was more convinced than ever that no one from Yallaroo had ever amounted to much.

Her father kissed her goodnight. Ally turned off her light, rolled over, and peered out the window at the distant stars. They were bright and crisp in the cloudless spring night.

'Amazing,' she said softly.

**ALLY PULLED** on the rope with all her might.

Sports afternoon was on Fridays, and Mr Gibson had arranged an end-of-day tug of war between the year sevens and year eights. Tied to the middle of the rope was a red scarf. Two lines were drawn in chalk on the ground below. The goal was to pull the scarf over the line closest to your side.

'Ugg!'

'Oof!'

'Ugg!'

'Oof!'

Nothing had happened for more than two minutes.

The red scarf was stuck in the middle, first moving one way and then the other.

'Listen!' Jamie whispered so the others could hear. 'Let go of the rope when I give the word.'

'That's a stupid idea,' Bill Tommetti said. 'They'll win!'

Ally could see what Jamie had in mind. 'Just do it!' she snapped. 'It'll work!'

They strained on the rope for another moment.

'Now!' Jamie yelled.

As they let go of the rope, the year eights fell backwards in a sprawling heap. At the same moment, Jamie and the others grabbed the rope again and pulled hard. Within seconds they had dragged the red scarf across the line.

As they all cheered, Ally slapped palms with Jamie. 'Good thinking,' she congratulated him, and he gave her a bashful smile.

The school bell rang and they all grabbed their bags and headed for the school bus. Jamie sat in the seat in front of Ally and they continued to chat. Ping and Harmony climbed on, saw who she was talking to, and sat further down the bus. They made *kissy-kissy* motions at Ally with their lips.

Ally ignored them.

'How's your science project going?' Jamie asked.

Ally didn't immediately answer. She'd been talking to Harmony and Ping about it all week. They'd had plenty of ideas, but lots of arguments too. Ping had suggested they play various sorts of music to plants to see how they responded, or roll a dice thousands of times to see if any numbers were rolled more than others.

The ideas sounded boring to Harmony, and she'd told Ping as nicely as possible that she'd rather eat rat poison.

Harmony's idea was to build an exploding volcano to see what kinds of rocks were thrown the furthest. She had an uncle who owned a construction company, and she thought she could borrow some boxes of dynamite. Ally thought they had a better chance of being arrested as terrorists than winning the contest.

'It's going fine,' Ally said noncommittally to Jamie. 'We've still got to iron out a few details.'

'Do you have a name for your group yet?'

'Not yet.' Every team entering the contest had to come up with a name. 'We've got a few. We should have it by Monday.'

*I hope*, she thought.

Even deciding on a name had been difficult. They had come up with many: the Einsteins, the Frankensteins, the Volcanic Eruptions (one of Harmony's suggestions), the Plant Growers (one of Ping's ideas), the Science Girls, and the much argued suggestion of the I Hate Barbie team (another Harmony idea).

'Any plans for the weekend?' Jamie asked casually.

'It's Ping's birthday.'

'Oh.' He paused. 'Anything else?'

She was about to say no when the Tommetti triplets climbed onto the bus.

'Hey, Jamie!' Ben said. 'You talking to your girlfriend?'

Jamie turned around. 'She's not my girlfriend,' he said.

'She's got red hair like you!' Bill said.

Jamie turned back to look at Ally. Feigning surprise, he said, 'Wow! Your hair is red. Like, really red. I hadn't noticed.'

Ally's eyes opened wide. 'Hey! Yours too!'

'Who knew?'

'You two are so dumb,' Bob said.

The triplets headed for the back of the bus. The

driver started the engine and the bus clattered down the road.

'I so hate those guys,' Ally said.

'You should feel sorry for them,' Jamie said. 'Their mother died when they were only babies.'

'I didn't know that.'

'It was terrible. She fell out of a hot air balloon while on an African safari.'

*Wow*, Ally thought. *How awful.*

'She might have survived,' Jamie said, 'except she then got trampled by a rhinoceros.'

She punched him in the arm. 'You just made all that up,' she said.

'Yes. Their mum ran off with a used-car salesman. She lives in Bendigo.'

'That I can believe.'

'Although she's since had another set of triplets.'

Another set of triplets? Ally tried to imagine three more Tommetti triplets let loose on the world. 'Really?' she said.

'No. I made up that up too.'

Ally punched him in the arm again as he burst out laughing.

The bus reached Jamie's stop and he climbed off.

Harmony and Ping slid into the seats around Ally.

'You and Jamie,' Harmony said. 'I knew it.'

'You're ridiculous.'

'Have you decided how many children you're having?' Ping asked. 'Two or three? Or more? Six or seven? Or—'

'He's just a friend. Besides,' Ally added, 'my first love is science.'

They reached Ally's stop and she got off. As the bus pulled away, she looked back to see Harmony and Ping making *kissy-kissy* faces against the glass.

She sighed.

*Idiots!*

**'HOW'S THE** science project?' Ally's dad asked.

Ally had been sitting at her desk working on a history assignment when her dad popped his head in the door. He had a smear of grease on his cheek. She grabbed a tissue and wiped it off.

'We're making progress,' she said.

'Which means you haven't got anywhere.'

Ally sighed. 'That's about right,' she admitted.

They were running out of time. Soon, they had to let their class know what experiment they planned to carry out, as well as submit the application form for the contest.

'What's the problem?'

'We can't agree on anything,' Ally said, telling him some of the ideas they'd had. 'And everything already seems to have been discovered.'

'You're meant to be demonstrating the scientific method,' Russell said. 'That doesn't necessarily mean you're discovering anything new. You could just find a way to prove something that most people know, but take for granted.'

'What do you mean?'

'Well,' Russell said, sitting on the edge of her bed. 'Do you know how an incandescent light bulb works?'

'Uh...' Ally thought for a moment. 'Not really.'

'Light bulbs are mostly just a globe and a filament. The globe is the glass bulb, and the filament is a wire thread that sits in the middle. It's the filament that produces light. Electricity passes through most metals fairly well, but not through things like wood or rubber.

'The filament of a typical light bulb is made of tungsten metal, which conducts electricity, but resists it to the point where it glows white-hot. This white-hot glow is the light produced by the bulb. To make the filament last longer, the inside of a light bulb contains an inert gas, usually a gas called argon.

'This is why these old-style incandescent light bulbs are being phased out. A lot of the energy they produce is lost as heat. Most modern lights are a different kind: fluorescent or LED.' He paused. 'We see the wonders of science around us every day, but we take them for granted because they're so commonplace.'

Ally thought about this. 'So you think we should just try to prove something simple?' she said.

'Sure. When people don't understand something, they often make up their own explanation for it. Or, sometimes, they flat out deny that it's even real.'

'What do you mean?'

Russell rubbed his chin. 'Well,' he said, 'there are people who don't believe we ever went to the moon.'

'Oh,' Ally laughed. 'I read about that.'

'Why are you laughing? How do *you* know that astronauts landed on the moon?'

'What? You're not saying you doubt it?' she said.

'Of course not,' he said. 'It's one of humankind's greatest achievements. Especially using the technology they had at the time.' He paused. 'But it's easy to laugh at conspiracy theorists. The important thing is to prove it to yourself. So how do you know it happened?'

'Well,' Ally said slowly, 'there's all the television footage.'

'That could be faked.'

'That seems pretty unlikely,' Ally said. 'There were thousands of people involved in launching the spaceships. If the moon landings were faked, then it means that all those people were lying.'

Russell nodded. 'That's good thinking,' he said. 'But let's assume for a moment that everyone involved in sending those men to the moon was *really* good at keeping a secret. How else could we prove it had really happened?'

Ally sighed. 'I'm not sure,' she finally said. 'How?'

'There are a couple of ways. First of all, the Apollo astronauts brought back a lot of moon rock. Over three hundred kilograms. Much of this rock was donated to countries all over the world. There are a few pieces in Canberra.

'The rock was independently tested and found to be completely different to what we find here on Earth.'

'And what else?' Ally asked.

'The Apollo astronauts left a retroreflector array—a panel of mirrors—on the moon,' Russell said. 'Even today, astronomers can fire a laser at the moon and the special mirrors bounce the signal right back.'

'And anything else?'

'Unmanned spacecraft have been sent to orbit the moon since the original landings,' Russell said. 'They've photographed the surface and actually filmed the tracks left by the astronauts.'

'Their footsteps are still there?' she asked. 'Haven't they been worn away?'

'By what?' Russell smiled. 'Remember, there's no wind or rain on the moon. Those footsteps will be there forever.'

'Dad,' Ally said, 'how did you ever get to be so smart?'

'Not just smart,' he said, winking. 'But also a great artist.'

'If you say so.'

Ally smiled. Russell said goodnight, and she got ready for bed. Turning out her light, Ally opened her blind, and watched the full moon rising above the horizon.

*People have walked there*, she thought. *Incredible*.

That night, her dreams were full of flying to the moon and following in the footsteps of the brave men who had first walked there.

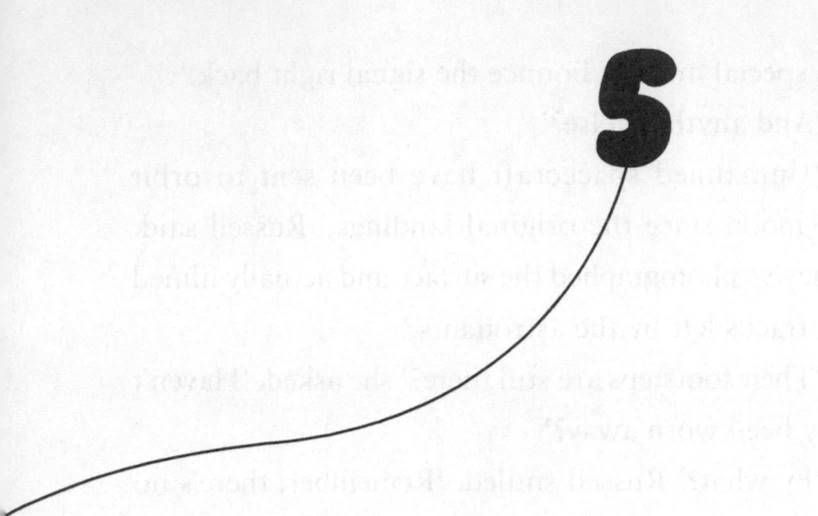

# 5

**'TO YOUR** left!' Ally yelled. 'No! I mean your other left!'

'Right!' Harmony yelled. 'Further up! No! Down!'

Ping's party was in full swing. Music was playing. Kids were running around. The backyard was full of people. Most of them were family who had come to celebrate. A lot of them were younger cousins. They were all yelling advice to Ping, who was blindfolded and trying to hit a donkey-shaped piñata hanging from a tree.

Ping hit its tail twice, but the tree multiple times. Ally was laughing so hard she was almost doubled over.

Finally, Ping gave one almighty swing of the bat and sent the piñata flying. Shattering, it sent a shower of wrapped lollies everywhere. Ping dragged off the blindfold and threw it to the ground as the little kids swarmed around her.

'They're like zombies,' Harmony said, watching them fight for the winnings.

'They'd eat anything,' Ping agreed. 'Even us.'

'Which reminds me,' Harmony continued, 'how do you feel about Zombie Death Eaters as a name for our team?'

'It's very...memorable,' Ally said.

At that moment, Mrs Chong appeared with a cake and called everyone together to sing 'Happy Birthday'. Visitors gathered around as she stepped forward. 'Our little girl Ping is thirteen years old today,' she said. 'We are very proud of her.'

Everyone sang, then cheered as Ping blew out the candles. Her mother cut the cake, and her father handed it around.

'You're good girls,' Mr Chong said to Ally and Harmony as he offered them a piece. 'Interested in school. You study hard. Do well. Like our Ping,' he said proudly. 'She's going to be a doctor, like her mother.'

Ping rolled her eyes at Ally and Harmony. She had no interest in being a doctor, and they both knew it.

After they'd eaten their cake, Ping took the two girls aside. 'There's something I need to show you,' she said.

She led them inside. Ping's home was nothing like Ally's place. It was immaculate.

'Your place is always so clean,' Ally said, admiringly.

'My mum vacuums twice a day,' Ping said.

'Twice a day!' Ally said. 'We haven't vacuumed in months.'

'No time?'

'Can't find the vacuum cleaner.'

'I'm not sure we ever vacuum,' Harmony said. 'My mother doesn't like to kill anything. Even dust mites. One day I saw her taking an ant outside.' Ping's room was as clean and tidy as the rest of the house, but here the walls were covered with framed posters. One was of the Sydney Harbour Bridge. Another was of the Golden Gate Bridge. A third was Tower Bridge in London.

'You haven't seen this one,' Ping said, pointing to a picture in the corner. 'It's the Akashi Kaikyō Bridge in Japan.'

Ping was a pontist—she loved anything to do with bridges.

'That's...great,' Ally said.

'Stimulating,' Harmony said.

Ping took her schoolbag from its hook on the back of the door and produced a sheet of paper from it. 'I found this in my bag yesterday,' she said, holding it out so they could read it:

*Dont enter the siens contest. Or else*

There was a skull and crossbones drawn at the bottom.

'Wow,' Harmony said, approvingly. 'A threatening letter.'

'And almost in English,' Ally said.

'I've made a list of who I think could have sent it,' Ping said, going to her desk. She pulled out several sheets of paper.

'Ping,' Harmony said, 'how many people are on this list?'

'Three hundred and forty-eight.'

'There's only three hundred and fifty students in the entire school.'

'That's right,' Ping said. 'I've ruled out you and Harmony because you're my friends.'

‘Ping,’ Ally said, ‘I think it’s pretty obvious who it’s from.’

‘It’s from the Tommetti triplets,’ Harmony said. ‘But why?’

‘Surely they’re not entering the science contest,’ Ally said. ‘They don’t even know how to *spell* science.’

‘They don’t read books,’ Ping said. ‘One day I heard Ben say that books are only good for starting fires.’

‘Idiots,’ Harmony seethed.

‘Relax,’ Ally said. ‘We’ve got nothing to worry about. Those boys won’t do anything. And they’re not going to win anyway.’

The girls heard a cry from the backyard. Going to the window, they pushed the curtain aside and looked out. A little girl, one of Ping’s cousins, was bawling her eyes out. Her red balloon was flying up into the sky.

Ally watched the balloon. It rounded a tree in the backyard, was caught by an updraft and zoomed upwards, its string glittering in the sunlight. The wind took it higher and higher until it was a tiny red dot in the clear blue sky.

‘That’s it,’ Ally breathed.

The other girls frowned.

'What?' Harmony asked.

'I know what we'll do for our science project,' Ally said.

# 6

**ALLY ARRANGED** for Harmony and Ping to come to her place the next afternoon. She made an effort to clean the house, but it needed a bulldozer and not a broom.

Her father had been working on a broken-down harvester. 'You don't need to tidy up for your friends,' he said. 'They like you just as you are.'

'I know,' Ally said. 'I'm just checking where everything is so I'll know where to look if Ping and Harmony go missing.'

'Ha, ha,' Russell said. 'Just make certain they're careful in the bathroom. I've just hung a new painting in there.'

'I'll warn them. Are you going somewhere?'

'I'm off to pick up an excavator.'

'Can it be fixed?'

'You can never have enough rusting wrecks in your backyard.'

'Great to know.'

Ping and Harmony arrived soon after he left. They always told Ally that they loved her house, though she wasn't sure how they could. Winston greeted them with a flurry of barks.

Harmony, always ready to blow anyone up or feed them to zombies, was helpless in Winston's presence. 'You little goo goo puppy wuppy,' she crooned, picking up Winston. 'I wuv you sooooooo much.'

'Amazing,' Ping said. 'This is the girl who'd destroy Yallaroo without thinking twice about it.'

Shaking her head, Ally led them to her room. 'Okay,' she said as they sat on her bed. 'Thanks for coming here today.'

'We didn't have a choice,' Harmony said. 'You refused to tell us your brilliant idea.'

Ally took a deep breath. 'Let me ask you a question. Is the Earth flat or is it round?'

'Let me ask *you* a question,' Harmony said. 'Did you hit your head recently?'

'Just tell me—is the Earth flat or round?'

'It's round,' Ping said. 'Although it's not completely round, because it bulges a bit at the sides. Not a lot. Just a little. Not as much—'

'How do you know it's round?' Ally interrupted.

'Well...' Ping thought for a long moment. 'Astronauts have flown into space. There's film that shows the Earth is round. Then there are satellites. Plus the International Space Station.'

'But what if all that were faked?'

Harmony was staring at her. 'Have you felt any brain pain?' she asked. 'They found a guy in India who had a worm in his head. Have you heard any digging recently?'

'My brain is fine,' Ally said. 'Anyway, what evidence is there that the world is round?'

'I'm sure there's lots of evidence,' Harmony said, 'although I'm not sure what it is. But why are you asking? Everyone knows the world is round.'

'Not everyone,' Ally said. 'There's a growing number of people who believe the Earth is flat. Thousands of people, actually.'

'Why? How?' Harmony was speechless. 'What?'

Ally shrugged. 'Anyone can use social media,' she said. 'They can use it to stay in touch with friends, or they can also use it to promote weird and bizarre ideas—like that the moon landings never happened, or that dinosaurs helped build the pyramids, or that chemicals in the water are used to brainwash us.'

Winston gave a woof.

'See,' Ally said. 'Even Winston thinks it's silly.'

'So what's the evidence?' Ping asked. 'That the Earth is round, I mean.'

'Okay,' Ally said, nodding. She'd been reading up on this since Ping's party. 'There's lots of evidence, and it can be found by ordinary people like us. First of all, if you stand on a beach and watch a ship heading out over the horizon, it doesn't just get smaller and smaller. It slowly sinks from sight. That's because it's disappearing below the horizon, like a bug disappearing over the edge of a ball.'

'I know what you mean,' Harmony said. 'I noticed that when mum and I went to Cape Otway for a holiday.'

'Also, the night sky viewed from Australia is different to the night sky in, say, America. It's because the Southern and Northern Hemispheres are aimed at different parts of the universe. If the Earth were flat, you'd see the same stars from both locations.'

'That's pretty good thinking,' Ping said. 'What else?'

'Okay, you remember what a lunar eclipse is?'

Ping frowned. 'Sure,' she said. 'It's when the Earth passes between the moon and the sun. You can see the shadow of the Earth move across the moon's surface.'

'There was that one last year,' Harmony said. 'Half the town went to Hanley Hill to see it.'

'And what was the shape of that shadow?'

Ping sat up straight. 'It was curved!' she said. 'But how does all that help us? We need to carry out some kind of experiment where we can hand in actual evidence.'

'That's true,' Harmony said. 'We can't stage a lunar eclipse or fly overseas. And the nearest beach is hours away.'

'You're right,' Ally said, 'so I've got something exciting in mind.' She paused. 'I think we should go to space.'

The other girls didn't speak for a moment.

'Okay,' Harmony finally said. 'We're going to space. We'll build a rocket ship. Go to the moon.

Maybe have some green cheese while we're there. Pick up some hot alien guys. Catch a comet to Jupiter—'

'We can't go to space,' Ping said. 'It would cost billions of dollars.'

Ally shook her head. 'I don't mean that we're personally going to space. We'll attach a video camera to a balloon, send it up really high, and film its journey. It'll show the curvature of the Earth, and that'll prove the Earth is round.'

'Balloons can't go up that high,' Harmony said. 'Can they?'

'Weather balloons can,' Ally said. 'All we have to do is fill the balloon with helium and stick a camera on it. It'll be easy!'

'Really?' Ping asked.

'Maybe not that easy,' Ally admitted. 'Still, we'll have a good chance of winning.'

Winston barked in agreement.

'Well,' Harmony said, 'we have to give our presentation to Miss Kapoor this week as well as submit our application.'

'We can do it,' Ping said. 'This will be amazing!'

There was the sound of a car from next door. Ally went to the window and pushed the curtain aside.

A hearse had just pulled into Mrs Blunt's driveway. It had a single bench seat in the front and little curtains in the back to hide the coffin.

'What?' she said. 'Don't tell me old Mrs Blunt is dead!'

The others crowded around the window. 'Is that bad news?' Harmony asked.

'Wanting people dead isn't nice,' Ally said. 'Even when it's Mrs Blunt.'

'The back looks like it's already full,' Ping said. 'Is Mrs Blunt having a body delivered?'

'Only if she eats dead people,' Harmony said. 'Which is a real possibility.'

The driver's door opened and a short, pale man stepped out.

'I know who that is,' Ping said. 'He just bought the funeral home. His name's Arthur Drake. His business is near mum's medical centre.'

Mr Drake knocked at Mrs Blunt's front door. It opened, and Mrs Blunt followed him out to his car. He went to the rear and opened the doors.

'That's bizarre,' Ally said. 'He's showing off his coffin to her.'

'Maybe he's a vampire,' Harmony said.

'There's no such thing as vampires,' Ally said. 'Or zombies or ghosts or anything like that.'

'There's Hicky Saw.'

Ally sighed. 'Hicky Saw isn't real,' she said.

'I don't know,' Harmony said. 'I know someone who saw him.'

'Really?'

'Look!' Ping urged.

Drake reached into the back of the hearse, but instead of pulling out a coffin or a dead body, he lifted out a bunch of flowers.

'What?' Harmony said. 'He's delivering flowers to her?'

'Maybe he stole them from a grave,' Ping said.

Then Mrs Blunt did something that Ally had never seen her do before. An odd expression crossed her face as she took them from Mr Drake. She twirled a strand of hair between her fingertips as she laughed.

'It's a gift,' Ally said. 'They're going on a date.'

'What?' the other girls shrieked.

They were so loud that Mrs Blunt and Mr Drake glanced up at their window. Ally dragged Ping and Harmony behind the curtains. When they peeked out again, they saw that Mrs Blunt was pointing to their house.

'I think she's saying something nasty about you,' Ping said.

'Typical,' Ally said.

Mrs Blunt disappeared inside with the flowers.

'Maybe Mrs Blunt is under some kind of spell,' Harmony said. 'Dracula can mesmerise people. He has brides that he sends out to fetch young children to feed his blood lust.'

Oddly, Ally didn't find it hard to imagine Mrs Blunt feeding young children to her vampire boyfriend.

Mrs Blunt reappeared after a few minutes.

'Look how she's dressed,' Ping said.

The older woman had quickly changed into a flowing black dress and a white shawl.

'That's vampire clothing if ever I saw it,' Harmony said.

The couple climbed into Mr Drake's car and drove off.

'There they go,' Harmony said. 'Off to drink the blood of the young children of Yallaroo.'

'Never mind them,' Ally said. 'We need to get busy. We're going to space.'

**'NOW,' MISS** Kapoor said. 'I'd like to see what everyone has planned for their science project.'

Ben, Bob and Bill all raised their hands.

'Yes?' Miss Kapoor said.

'Please, miss,' Ben said. 'Can we go first?'

'You may. What is your team name?'

'We're the Save the Earth from the Lizard People team,' Bill said.

'I see,' Miss Kapoor said, although it was obvious she didn't see at all. 'Perhaps it's best if you simply explain your project and we can discuss the name later.'

The boys went to the front of the room.

'Thousands of years ago,' Bob started, 'the world was very different. There was no internet. There were no cars. There were no new television shows. Only re-runs. People wore different clothing to what they wear today—mostly animal skins.'

He paused to let this sink in.

'In those days, the world was run by two races: humans and lizard people,' Bob said.

'Are you talking about dinosaurs?' Miss Kapoor asked.

'No.' Bob allowed the word to hang in the air. 'This was a different race entirely. There were dinosaurs, lizard people, and people people.'

'Dinosaurs and humans weren't around at the same time. You remember we covered that in class last term?'

'They weren't living in the same place,' Bob said. 'People lived in houses, and dinosaurs lived in the wild.'

'No. They appeared at different times in history. Dinosaurs died out over sixty million years ago. Early humans appeared around two million years ago.'

'Anyway,' Bob said, ignoring her, 'lizard people have lived alongside us in secret for thousands of years.

Many ancient cultures—the Egyptians, Greeks and Romans—worshipped lizard people. This is because lizard people walked among us.' He paused dramatically. 'And they still do.'

This amazing revelation was greeted by a long silence.

'Bob,' Miss Kapoor finally said. 'I haven't seen any lizard people of late.'

'They wear disguises, so they look like us,' he said. 'And they hold positions of great power. They're business leaders, members of the royal family, political leaders. Just look at our prime minister. He's obviously a lizard person.'

Miss Kapoor sighed. 'Bob,' she said, 'the point of the contest is to use the scientific method. The first step is to work out what you want to know. In this case, the question you're asking is: *Do lizard people exist?* Then you need to gather information.'

Ben held up a book. 'We've done research,' he said.

The book was a battered paperback titled *Lizard People Live Among Us*, and it was written by someone named T. J. Smith. The picture on the front showed a man pulling off a rubber mask to reveal a lizard face beneath. A woman was recoiling from him in horror.

Bob opened the book to reveal a grainy black-and-white image of a person with a lizard face. 'This is Albert Einstein,' he said. 'He was a lizard person.'

'Albert Einstein was not a lizard person!' Ally said.

Miss Kapoor held up a hand. 'You can't just use information from a single book, or source on the internet. You need to gather data from a variety of resources. After doing this, you need to form your hypothesis, which might be: if lizard people are real, then we should be able to gather some photographic evidence.' She turned to the class. 'Does anyone have any thoughts about what other experiments the boys could carry out?'

'Find lizard people footprints,' Charlotte suggested.

'And what else?'

'Set a trap to catch a lizard person,' Bruce said.

'Cool,' Bill enthused.

'And if you should successfully gather such evidence?' Miss Kapoor asked.

'Draw a conclusion,' Ally said.

'Exactly,' Miss Kapoor said. 'In this case it means deciding if your original hypothesis was correct or not. In your case: *Do lizard people exist?*' She sent the boys back to their desks and examined the triplets' application form. 'This seems to be in order, such as it is. All right, who's next?'

Jamie, Bruce and Charlotte went to the front of the classroom. They loaded up their slide display, and a picture of a beehive appeared on the screen.

'Bees are one of nature's smallest but most important creatures,' Jamie began. 'They collect pollen and nectar. As they fly from flower to flower, they spread the pollen and this fertilises plants. The nectar is taken back to the hive where it is processed into honey.'

Charlotte continued. 'There are over fifteen hundred types of native Australian bees,' she said. 'But bees are in trouble. Their numbers are in decline all over the country. Pesticides poison bees' food supplies, and the continual growth of urban areas destroys their natural environments.'

'There's also the problem that our cities and suburbs don't produce a lot of flowers,' Bruce said. 'Fewer flowers means fewer bees.'

'Flowers,' Bill snickered.

'Native bees are essential to human survival,' Charlotte said, glaring at him. 'They pollinate many kinds of Australian fruits and vegetables.'

'Our plan is to help the bees,' Jamie said. 'We're going to plant different types of flowering shrubs around Yallaroo. In some places we'll use native plants; in others we'll use European plants. We're going to work out which types of flowers are the most successful at attracting bees. If you can attract more bees, you improve their chances of survival—and ours as well.'

Miss Kapoor was nodding enthusiastically. 'What are you calling your team?' she asked.

'The Busy Bees,' Jamie said.

Ally heard Bill Tommetti whisper to one of his brothers. 'Bees,' he said. 'So boring.'

'Lizard people are way more exciting,' Bob agreed.

Next it was time for Ally's team to present. She began by explaining that a growing number of people were convinced that the world was flat.

'There's a lot of dummies around,' Ben Tommetti said loudly.

'Shh,' Miss Kapoor said.

Ping and Harmony went on to detail their plan: they intended to launch three balloons. They would do it over a period of weeks just in case the weather was bad or there were unforeseen problems along the way. Each of the balloons would film the earth from above, and hopefully capture the curvature of the horizon, proving that the world was round.

'How high will they go?' Miss Kapoor asked.

'They'll reach a height of about thirty-five kilometres,' Harmony said.

Bruce raised his hand. 'That doesn't sound very high,' he said. 'That's only the distance from Yallaroo to Benalla.'

Ally had been reading about this. 'It's hardly any distance at all—on the ground,' she said, 'but we forget how little atmosphere we have surrounding the Earth. It's a really thin shell. If you shrunk the Earth down to the size of an apple, the atmosphere would only be as thick as the apple's skin.'

Harmony continued. 'The area we live in is called the troposphere,' she said. 'Above that is the stratosphere—planes fly at that level—then the mesosphere, thermosphere and the exosphere. When you get to those higher levels, you're in outer space.'

'How high is that?' Miss Kapoor asked.

'About a hundred kilometres up.'

'And where are your balloons going?'

'Only as far as the stratosphere. But that's high

enough to show that the Earth is round.'

Everyone looked interested—everyone, except the Tommetti triplets.

'What a stupid idea,' Ben said. 'That'll cost a million dollars to do.'

Before Ally could say anything, Jamie spun around. 'Why don't you shut up?' he snapped.

'It's not my fault your girlfriend's a balloon,' Ben said.

Both boys started yelling at each other until Miss Kapoor shushed them into silence.

'What's the name of your team?' Miss Kapoor asked as Ally's team sat down.

'Our name?' Ally repeated.

In all their preparations, they'd forgotten about coming up with a name. Ally glanced helplessly at Ping and Harmony.

'It's...uh...' Harmony began.

'We're the...' Ping faltered.

'Balloon...' Ally started, her mind racing, '...girls. We're the Balloon Girls!'

'Balloon Girls!' Bill Tommetti snorted. 'That's about right!'

'Silence!' Miss Kapoor said and turned to Ally's team. 'That sounds like an ambitious project. Do you know how much it's going to cost? You know you have to raise your own funds?'

Ally hadn't actually thought about this. 'We're working on that,' she said.

# 8

**'FIVE HUNDRED** dollars,' Ping said, thoughtfully. 'That's a lot of money.'

'Why does it cost so much?' Harmony asked. 'What do we get for five hundred dollars?'

They were back in Ally's bedroom. Ally was pleased to see they weren't too horrified by the figure. She'd been worried when she worked out the total amount.

'Some of the figures are guesses,' she explained, 'because we've got to make some of the things we need ourselves. But that should be fun anyway, like that time we made the model of the Sydney Opera House. Remember that?'

'I got to blow it up later,' Harmony said, wistfully. 'Good times.'

'So,' Ally continued, 'what we need are three weather balloons, helium, a camera, a gondola, a parachute for the camera, and a GPS that measures height, speed and distance.'

'Fine,' Harmony said. 'I have just one question—what are all those things?'

Ally nodded. 'I'll start with the basics,' she said. 'We need helium for the balloons.'

'Didn't helium make that old airship thingy explode?'

'You're thinking of the *Hindenburg*,' Ping said. 'It was an airship that exploded ages ago in New Jersey, America. Airships back then didn't use helium. They used hydrogen, which is highly explosive. Helium is completely safe. It's the same gas in party balloons.'

'Like the ones at your party,' Ally added. 'Nothing's exploding in our experiment.'

'And the other things?' Harmony asked.

'We need a camera to record the balloon's journey, as evidence. We also need a gondola to hold the camera.'

'Like a little basket?' Ping said.

'It may or may not be a basket. It just needs to be as light as possible.'

'And you mentioned a GSP…' Harmony said.

'GPS,' Ally corrected her. 'It stands for global positioning system. It will send a signal back to our laptop that tells us the balloon's height and speed, and the distance it's travelled. It'll also help us find the gondola after the balloon explodes.'

'I thought you said nothing was exploding,' Ping said.

'Well, it just pops really. The air pressure drops as the balloon rises. The helium inside the balloon expands, stretching the balloon out so it gets bigger and bigger until it finally bursts and falls to Earth.'

Harmony was nodding. 'Okay,' she said. 'I can see why we need a tracking device. And the parachute stops the gondola from smashing to pieces when it hits the ground?'

'It does. We'll be making the parachute from a super-light fabric. Probably nylon.'

'I can do that,' Ping offered.

Ally nodded. She was hoping Ping would make the parachute; she had done a great job of making their costumes for the school play the previous term.

'I just have one last question,' Harmony said.

'What is it?'

'It was common to use animals as test pilots in the early days of space. Can we use the Tommetti triplets?'

'That's a fantastic idea,' Ally agreed. 'Though I should point out that the temperature will get down to minus fifty, and it would be impossible for them to breathe.'

'And the problem is…?'

'It's too expensive,' Ally added. 'Otherwise, it's a perfectly fine idea.'

The girls spent the next hour talking about ways they could raise the five hundred dollars, but they were unable to settle on anything. Ally suggested they sleep on it.

Reaching the front door, they were just in time to see Mr Drake's car pull into Mrs Blunt's driveway. They eased the door open to eavesdrop.

'My dear,' Mr Drake said as they strolled to her house, 'I've had a lovely evening.'

'Arthur,' Mrs Blunt said, pushing her hair back, 'I enjoyed it too.'

The funeral director took Mrs Blunt's hand and gave it a kiss. She tittered.

'Oh Arthur!' she said. 'You're incorrigible!'

Harmony nudged Ally. 'What does incorrigible mean?' she asked.

'Something to do with corrugated iron?'

'I can't see any bite marks,' Ping whispered.

'Bite marks?' Ally said.

'On her neck.'

Ally peered closer. It was true: Mrs Blunt's neck was unblemished. Whatever control Mr Drake had over her had nothing do with vampirism.

The odd couple entered Mrs Blunt's house.

'Could it be that they're in...' Ping's voice trailed off.

'What?' Ally said.

'You know...love?'

# 9

**AFTER THE** girls had gone home, Ally read for a while before going to bed. She was in a deep sleep when she was awakened by Winston's barking.

'Be quiet,' she muttered.

He jumped onto her bed and sat on her chest. Groaning, she pushed him off and looked at her clock.

'Winston,' she said. 'It's one in the morning. Go back to sleep.'

But the little dog continued to bark.

'What is it?' she asked, sitting up.

She snapped on her bedroom lamp. Winston raced to the door, stopped to look back at her and whined.

Ally sighed. 'All right,' she said.

She climbed out of bed and followed him through the house to the back.

'What is it?' Ally whispered, easing open the back door. 'A fox?'

Foxes were a pest. A tall wire fence surrounded their property, but foxes sometimes crawled under it searching for food.

She looked out. The moon was a pale smudge in the sky, but Ally could see well enough to make out the workshop, and the skeletal remains of the farming equipment in the darkness. A cool wind was clanging a loose piece of metal.

Barking wildly, Winston charged out into the night.

'Winston!' Ally snapped.

She went racing after him, manoeuvring around the huge pieces of farm equipment. Winston disappeared behind an old tractor.

'Winston!' Ally yelled. 'Stop!'

The little dog gave a high-pitched cry—and fell silent.

'Winston?' she said.

Another piece of metal clattered nearby, and she was suddenly aware that she was out here alone. Her father was sound asleep in bed. No one could get through the fence unless they were...a ghost.

Hicky Saw wasn't real. He wasn't searching Yallaroo for people whose arms and legs he could sever. That was just a story.

Wasn't it?

'Winston?' Ally squeaked.

There was frantic barking, and Winston came tearing around the corner and leapt into her arms. Ally turned and ran with him back to the house.

Inside, she saw that Winston had blood around his mouth—and a scrap of cloth.

*Someone was out there!*

She woke her father. He went outside armed with an iron bar and a torch, but returned a short time later.

'There's no one out there,' he said. 'Are you sure you didn't imagine—'

'I did not,' Ally said firmly. 'And what about the bloody cloth?

They went back to bed, and the rest of the night passed without incident. Russell went out again the next morning, this time returning with a grim expression on his face.

'What is it?' Ally asked.

'I don't want to worry you,' he said.

'I'm already worried.'

She followed him to where Winston had disappeared behind the rusting farming machinery. A trail of blood led from where they stood to the fence, where a hole had been cut in the wire. On the other side was the road.

'We *did* have an intruder,' Russell said.

Winston woofed.

Ally gave him a pat. 'But why?' she asked. 'What were they doing?'

'Maybe trying to steal some stuff,' Russell said. 'Some kids tried a few years back.'

'In the middle of the night?'

Russell shrugged. 'Who knows,' he said. 'Maybe they were trying to steal one of my pictures. They'll be worth a lot of money one day.'

'I'm sure.'

On the school bus that morning, Ally told Harmony and Ping what had happened.

'It *must* be Hicky Saw,' Harmony said. 'You're lucky you still have arms and legs.'

'That's ridiculous,' Ally said. 'Ghosts aren't real.'

'Then who do you think it was?' Ping asked. 'And why would they be in your yard at night?'

Ally had no idea. 'Whoever it was,' she said, 'I don't think they got what they were after.'

'So they might come back.'

'You could set a trap,' Harmony said. 'Dig a trench just inside the fence line and fill it with crocodiles. Anyone who falls in will get eaten.'

'And who's digging this trench? And where do we find the crocodiles?'

'Details,' Harmony said airily.

The bus arrived at school, and they all piled out. The whole way in, the Tommetti triplets had been strangely quiet. Now Ally heard them sniggering as they raced off.

'What the—' she started.

A crude picture had been spray painted on the front wall of the school. It was obviously meant to be Ally, Ping and Harmony. Ally was impossibly fat, Harmony was wafer-thin, and Ping had been shown with a bamboo hat. Words were painted underneath: *Balloon Girls*.

Ally and the others exchanged glances. It was obvious who had created the hideous artwork: the

Tommetti triplets were laughing uproariously on the far side of the quadrangle.

'You idiots!' Harmony yelled. 'You're a bunch of morons!'

Ally clenched her fists tightly. 'They'll be sorry,' she muttered.

# 10

**THE GIRLS** submitted the application form for the ASEA contest, crossing their fingers that they'd be able to raise the money in time. By the time Friday rolled around, they still had no idea how they were going to do it. They arranged to meet the next morning at Moo Moo's Café on Clarke Street. Not only was Moo Moo's the hangout for most of Yallaroo, it also made the best milkshakes in the district.

Ally was already there when Ping and Harmony arrived not long after eight o'clock. It was still early, so there were only two other people at a table, a retired couple eating bacon and eggs.

Ally leaned in close as the others sat down. 'I have an idea for how to make money,' she whispered.

'Why are you whispering?' Ping asked.

'So no one hears us.'

'That's Mr and Mrs Mason,' Harmony said, indicating the elderly couple. 'They're both deaf. So what's your idea?'

Ally pointed out the window. 'What do you see there?' she asked.

They all looked out. The town wasn't exactly the centre of the universe. There were seventeen shops on the main street, but almost a quarter of them were permanently closed. Half-a-dozen vehicles were parallel-parked by the kerb. Mr Schwartz, the barber, was sweeping the front verandah of his shop. A lonely currawong on a street sign gave a rhythmic cry as a skinny stray dog meandered across the road.

'Not a lot,' Harmony said.

'But there's a lot of one thing,' Ally said. 'Dust.'

The girls looked again. A fine coating of dust covered everything. It hadn't rained in months.

'Yeah?' Harmony said.

'Everything needs a good clean,' Ally pointed out. 'Including cars.'

'And?' Ping said.

'We can wash cars!' Ally said. 'There are hundreds of cars in the district. We can charge five dollars a car. We'll have five hundred dollars before you know it!'

This suggestion was met with silence.

'Will people really pay money for us to do that?' Harmony asked.

'Of course they will,' Ally said. 'But there's one problem.'

'Only one?'

Ally grimaced. 'No one is allowed to use hoses to wash cars because of water restrictions,' she said. 'That means we'll have to do the whole thing with sponges and buckets. I've already spoken to Mr Whitely. He owns the garage on Anzac Road. He said we can use his spare shed to wash the cars.'

'It sounds like a lot of work,' Harmony said.

'Do you want to go to space or not?' Ally asked, exasperated.

'I should point out that *we're* not going to space,' Ping said. 'Only our balloon, and that's only going to the edge, anyway.'

'That's close enough.'

Ally had her mind set on making their fortune by washing cars and wouldn't be talked out of it. She said the first step was to advertise, so they decided to go to Harmony's place to make a flyer for people's letterboxes.

Harmony's home was a whitewashed weatherboard house close to the shops. The lawn was brown, but the wattle in the front yard was decorated with teapots and crystals. Wind chimes clanged on the front verandah. A scrawny cat lounged across the doorstep.

'Is that cat new?' Ping asked.

'That's Goldilocks,' Harmony confirmed. 'Mum found her behind the house.'

Her mum was famous for taking in stray cats. A lot of people had left town because of the drought, abandoning furniture, personal belongings and, worst of all, pets. Harmony's mum had made a point of taking them in.

'How many is that now?' Ally asked.

Harmony pushed open the front door, sending cats skittering in all directions.

'A lot,' she said. 'But she treats them all like family.'

Every inch of Harmony's bedroom was plastered with posters of Blood Guzzling Unicorns.

Harmony turned on her laptop. It only took a few minutes to put together a letterbox flyer. They examined the final result.

'I think that's okay,' Ally said.

The flyer read:

*Want your car washed?*

*We're washing cars this Saturday at Mr Whitely's garage to raise money for our science project.*

*We start at 8 am.*

*Your car will be amazingly spotless and clean!*

*It will be so clean you'll be able to eat off it!*

*Only $5!!!*

'I'm not sure about the "eating off the car" line,' Ping said. 'Is that hygienic?'

'They don't have to,' Harmony pointed out.

'I don't think we should use that line. We could get sued if they eat off their car and get sick.'

Sighing, Harmony deleted the line. They were able to print three flyers to a page on bright pink paper, but this meant they had to cut the pages into smaller sheets. This took hours. By the time they'd finished, they had several hundred.

'What now?' Harmony asked.

'Now we have to deliver them all around the town,' Ally said.

'It's too hot now,' Ping pointed out. The temperature had risen again and the street was baking outside.

Ally was keen to get going immediately, but Ping was right.

'All right,' she said. 'We'll do it tomorrow.'

**'ARE YOU** sure this is a good idea?' Ping asked.

It was recess and they were standing in the school quadrangle. It had taken Ally till Wednesday to come up with a plan to take revenge on the Tommetti triplets. Explaining it to the others, she found that Harmony was excited, but Ping was less thrilled.

'We have to do something!' Ally said. The faint image of them on the wall remained, despite the best efforts of the school cleaner. Every student had attended a compulsory antibullying session, but Ally was still annoyed. 'Injustice must be avenged!'

'I just don't want to get into trouble,' Ping said.

'We won't.'

They had to get to the classroom before their next class started. It was Mr Martin's English class, the first class after lunch. He was not one of Ally's favourite teachers—or anyone else's, for that matter. He was notoriously grumpy.

They made their way over to the classroom, a demountable at the rear of the school.

'Ping,' Ally said. 'Look normal.'

'I am looking normal,' Ping said.

She was walking as if she had two metal legs.

'That's not acting normal!' Harmony hissed.

'It's the best I can do! I'm not used to being a criminal!'

They went to the back of the building. Fortunately, the windows were open, but they were a few feet above the ground. The class was due to start soon, so the girls didn't have long. Ally reached into her schoolbag and took out a brush and a sealed tin.

'Give me a leg up,' she said.

Ping and Harmony formed a bridge with their hands and lifted her.

'Just a bit higher,' Ally said, gripping the windowsill. 'Just a bit more.'

The girls grunted and lifted her higher.

*Yes!*

She fell headfirst into the room.

*Oof!*

Ally rubbed her head, then pried open the tin and put her plan into action. It only took a few minutes to get everything ready. She was about to climb back out over the windowsill when she heard movement on the steps outside the door to the classroom.

*No!*

A key turned in the lock. Ally dove for the only hiding spot she could find—beneath the teacher's desk.

The door swung open, and Ally heard Mr Martin enter. Her heart was in her throat as he pottered about his desk. He pulled out his chair to sit down.

*This is terrible!* Ally thought.

At that moment Ally heard a voice at the door.

'Mr Martin?'

*Harmony!*

'Yes?' he said. 'We're not ready to start yet.'

'Oh.'

'Are you all right?' Mr Martin asked her.

'Oh...oh, yes,' Harmony said. 'I mean...no, there's something odd out here. I'm worried about it.'

'What is it?'

'Oh...a thing...'

'What kind of thing?' Mr Martin said, impatiently.

'Er...it's huge...strange...'

Ping poked her head around the doorframe. 'Like a spider,' she said.

Muttering, Mr Martin followed them. Ally sprinted to the window, tossed out the tin and brush, and jumped after them. Then, dusting herself off, she went to join the others on the verandah, where they were examining one of the corners.

'Well?' Mr Martin demanded. 'Where is it?'

'It was here a moment ago,' Harmony said.

'Maybe it flew off,' Ping said.

'Flew off?' Mr Martin said.

'It had wings,' Ping said, reddening. 'Small wings.'

The school bell rang, and Mr Martin told them to get to their seats. The rest of the class turned up not long after, including the Tommetti triplets, who took their usual seats at the rear.

'Let's see,' Mr Martin said, checking his roll. 'Whose turn is it this week?'

Every week a group of students had to get up and read a scene from the play they were studying—*The*

*Green Hills of Ciderville.* It was probably the most boring thing Ally had ever read.

'Ah ha,' Mr Martin said, referring to his roll. 'Bill, Ben and Bob. Come up, boys. We don't have all day.'

The boys made their way to the front.

There was a moment of shocked silence—and then the rest of the kids burst out laughing.

The boys looked about in confusion.

'What is it?' Bob asked.

Mr Martin frowned. 'Boys,' he said. 'Have you had an...accident?'

A brown smear was visible on the seats of their pants.

'What the—' Bill Tommetti yelled. 'It's paint!'

'Are you sure?' Mr Martin asked. 'Did you eat something that perhaps...'

'No!' Ben said. 'It's paint! It really is!'

Ally knew that too, as did Ping and Harmony, but they were careful to not look at each other.

'Well,' Mr Martin said, 'it'll dry quickly enough. Get on with the play.'

'But sir...sir...' Bob stammered. 'Can't we wash it out?'

'You can do that later. Don't think this will get you out of reading! This performance is part of your assessment!'

'But…we can't…we…' Bill started.

'The Green Hills await you!'

Red-faced, the triplets started reading their lines. Ben Tommetti looked up to see Ally and his eyes narrowed. Ally knew that he knew she had painted the seats of their chairs, but she didn't care. They deserved it!

It was Bob who got the biggest laugh as he read from the play. '…I wish I hadn't eaten that soup,' he said. 'I am feeling most unwell…'

# 12

**'RISE AND** shine!'

'Go away,' Ally groaned into her pillow. 'I need sleep.'

'What about the car wash?'

She sat bolt upright in bed. *The car wash!*

Her father was standing in the doorway. 'If you'd prefer to stay in bed all day…' he said, smiling.

'No!' Ally said. 'The car wash! Today's the day!'

She leapt out of bed and within minutes had showered, dressed, and eaten breakfast. As she finished off her toast, Winston gave her a hopeful bark.

'Sorry,' she said. 'No toast for dogs.'

'We'd better get moving,' Russell said.

Ally glanced at her watch. They were due to start at eight o'clock, and it was already seven-thirty!

Russell helped load her supplies of buckets, sponges and cleaning products into the back of the car. As they drove into town, he glanced back at them. 'Are you sure you've got enough cleaning liquid?' he asked.

'I think so,' she said. 'Why?'

'Well, five dollars is pretty cheap for a car wash.'

They hadn't really thought about the cost, Ally realised. They'd never organised a car wash before.

Anzac Road ran along the east side of town. It was usually pretty deserted—but today there was a traffic jam.

'Maybe there's been an accident,' Ally said, glancing over the bonnet.

'Hmm,' Russell said. 'I don't think so. We'll use the back lane.'

They entered the garage and found Harmony and Ping speaking with Mr Whitely. He was an elderly man with white hair and a stoop.

'I wasn't expecting this,' he was saying. 'Never seen anything like it.'

'What's going on?' Russell asked.

'That traffic jam,' Mr Whitely said. 'It's blocked the entire street.'

'What caused it?' Ally asked.

'We did!' Ping said.

'What?'

'They're lined up for car washes!' Harmony told her.

'Oh dear,' Ally said. 'Maybe we *are* too cheap.'

'Well, you can't change your price now,' Russell said. 'At least you won't be short of customers.'

He left, promising to return at five o'clock. Ally and the girls set themselves up in the shed adjacent to the garage. They filled buckets with water and lined up the sponges. The first car drove in as soon as Mr Whitely opened the front doors. It was someone from the local council.

'Lucky I got here early,' Councillor Barker said, emerging from her car. 'The street's completely blocked.'

The girls started at the front of her car and worked their way to the back. Reaching the roof was a problem, until the councillor suggested they use a chair. While they worked, she asked them what they were going to do with the money, and looked amazed when they explained.

'You're sending a balloon into space?' she said.

'Not quite space,' Ally said. 'But high enough to prove the world is round.'

'That's incredible. You girls should be very proud of yourselves.'

They thanked her as she paid and left.

'This is hard work,' Ping said.

'It'll be worth it,' Ally said.

'I hope so,' Harmony said. 'My volcano idea is looking better by the minute.'

As the next car pulled in, Ping looked past it and down the street.

'One down,' she said. 'Only a million to go.'

The day passed quickly. As soon as they finished one car, they had to move straight on to the next. The girls had brought their lunches, but ate as they worked. Ally and Ping had sandwiches, but Harmony's lunch was a vegan cheese salad.

'Does that taste okay?' Ally asked.

'Vegan cheese is improving all the time,' Harmony said diplomatically. 'It used to taste like old chewing gum.'

'And it doesn't anymore?'

'Not as much.'

Mr Whitely went out twice during the afternoon to get them more cleaning fluid. After a while they stopped checking the street—the line never seemed to get any shorter anyway.

The only oddity was when a long, black car pulled in.

Ally's mouth fell open.

*Mr Drake!*

He climbed out. '*You're* washing the cars?' he said. 'No wonder I've had to wait so long.'

'We're going as fast as we can,' Harmony said, coolly.

They got straight to work, not wanting to spend any more time with Mr Drake than necessary. Ally gulped as she checked the rear for a coffin.

*Thank goodness it's empty!* she thought.

Mr Drake suddenly stared at Ally. 'Don't you live on the other side of town?' he said. 'Your father has the tractor repair yard?'

'He repairs all sorts of farm equipment,' she said.

'I see.' He paused. 'Lived there long?'

She'd lived in the house her entire life.

'A while,' Ally said, warily.

'I've just moved to town,' he said. 'I was thinking about buying a house. Yours is an interesting example of the period.'

Ally wasn't sure what that meant—and didn't care anyway.

'Our house isn't for sale,' she said.

'I'll speak to your father,' Mr Drake said. 'I might be prepared to offer a good price.'

Ally kept her mouth shut. The girls finished washing his car, and were relieved when he left.

'What was that all about?' Ping asked.

'I don't know,' Ally said. 'It's all very odd.'

The line of cars finally evaporated around five o'clock. After the girls had tidied up and thanked Mr Whitely, Ally suggested they go back to her house to count the money. Russell drove them home.

By now Ally and the others were feeling more exhausted than they had in their entire lives. After showering and changing their clothes, Harmony tallied their money at the kitchen table, making piles of notes and coins while Russell made hot chocolate.

'I feel like I've been run over by a truck,' Ally groaned.

'Me too,' Ping agreed. 'Although it's more like a bus. Or maybe a tractor—'

'Don't be surprised if I fall asleep mid-counting,' Harmony said.

Russell handed them the steaming-hot mugs and a plate of biscuits.

'How's it looking?' he asked. 'It looks like you've made enough to get to Mars.'

'Hey,' Harmony said. 'This is *good*.'

'How much?' Ping and Ally asked simultaneously.

'Nine hundred and eighteen dollars!'

'That's fantastic!' Ally said. A lot of people had also donated money. 'We could send up ten balloons!'

'Three is enough—and we'll still have ice-cream money,' Harmony said.

'Harmony,' Ping said. 'That's a *lot* of ice cream.'

'I *like* ice cream.'

Ally cut in. 'Anyway,' she said, 'now we can order the equipment.'

Despite their exhaustion, they grouped around Ally's laptop and ordered the items needed. They bought three balloons, a camera, fabric for the parachute, a GPS, and hired the bottle of helium.

Russell smiled. 'I'm proud of you girls,' he said. 'You've done well.'

❧

The rest of the week passed slowly. Wednesday was sports day, and the girls were assigned to play volleyball on a team with the year eight girls. Harmony didn't like sport, Ally wasn't very fast, and Ping was too short. One of the older girls got annoyed when they were beaten.

'It's not our fault,' Ally said.

'Whose fault is it, then?' the girl asked.

The older girls marched off. Ally and the others retrieved their bags from the sidelines and started for the school bus.

Harmony frowned. 'That's weird,' she said.

'What is?' Ping asked.

'Something smells,' Harmony said.

Ally inhaled. There *was* a strange smell. Maybe it was road kill. Kangaroos and other wildlife sometimes got killed by passing cars, and it took a few days for the council to remove the bodies.

They headed home on the school bus. Jamie was sitting across the aisle from Ally, reading a book.

He glanced over at her. 'How's the science project coming?' he asked.

'Okay,' she said, and told him about the car wash.

'My dad told me about that. He had his car washed and said you did a good job.'

'We got pretty good at it,' she said. 'Practice does that.'

'You know,' Jamie said, 'the Twilight Movie festival is starting soon.'

The Twilight Movie series happened every year. Old films were projected onto the wall of Yallaroo's derelict jam factory. It was one of the biggest events of the year. Most of the town turned up, bringing deckchairs, stools, blankets and whatever else they could sit or lie on. An entry fee was charged, and the profits donated to the local district hospital.

'Is it?' Ally asked. 'Are you going?'

'I was thinking—'

A ball of paper bounced off the back of his head. He picked it up.

'Idiots,' he yelled, throwing it back at the Tommetti triplets.

The bus reached his stop, and he got out. As Ally watched him go, she heard the Tommetti triplets laughing at the back of the bus. She resisted the urge to yell at them herself.

'What's their problem?' she muttered to Ping and Harmony.

'I don't know,' Harmony said. 'They've been giggling ever since they got on the bus.'

Ally reached home and went on the internet for a while before doing some homework. She had a break when her dad called her to dinner. He had cooked one of her favourites—beef stroganoff.

'How long will it be till your gear arrives?' Russell asked.

'Only a few days for the GPS, the camera and the helium bottle. They're all coming from Melbourne. The balloons are from the US, though, so they'll take a few weeks.'

'Sounds like you're moving ahead.' He frowned. 'Have you checked the safety regulations?'

'What do you mean?'

'Well,' Russell said. 'You're launching a balloon that's going up really high. It could cross paths with an aeroplane. There must be some kind of safety regulations that say where and when you can launch balloons.'

'I hadn't thought about it,' Ally admitted. 'We don't want to cause an accident.'

'Have a look online and find out what you need to do.'

Gripped by a sudden panic, Ally went back to her bedroom and immediately started searching. Half an hour later she was able to sit back, feeling a little more relaxed.

They'd need to contact CASA—the Civil Aviation Safety Authority. The organisation handled all air safety issues in Australia. It looked like she just needed to get approval for the flights and keep CASA updated as to what happened on the day.

*What the—?*

There was that strange smell again. Had she stepped in something? She checked the bottom of her shoes. No.

*Where's it coming from?*

She opened her schoolbag and was hit by an overpowering stench.

Her schoolbooks fell out as she upended the bag. There was nothing strange about them. Taking a deep breath, she examined the inside. There was a lining at the bottom that pens and loose items sometimes slipped into. As she pushed it aside, a pale, silver object slid out.

*A dead fish!*

The stench was awful!

*How on Earth—?*

Ally's eyes narrowed. Filled with rage, she messaged Ping and Harmony telling them to check their bags. Dead fish had probably been hidden in their bags too.

*Those Tommetti triplets are going to be sorry!*

# 13

**'WE'VE GOT** to get some payback,' Harmony said. 'But how?'

They were sitting on a bench at the back of the school. It was lunchtime and the next class was history with Mrs Brogden.

'Where are the Tommettis now?' Ally asked.

'In the school library,' Ping said. 'I heard Ben say that they needed to start on their presentation for history.'

'Needed to start? Everyone's presenting this afternoon.'

'They can't write it in an hour,' Harmony said.

'I know how they do it,' Ping said. 'They cheat.'

'How?'

'They copy straight off the internet,' Ping said. 'I've seen them do it before.'

Ally's mind started to work. 'Let's head over there,' she said.

The library was fairly busy. Most of the students were in years eleven and twelve, studying or working on end-of-year assignments. The computer area was at the far end, behind some low-lying bookshelves.

The girls hid behind the nonfiction section.

'There they are,' Ally whispered.

The Tommettis were grouped around a monitor. Bill and Bob were giving instructions to Ben, who was copying and pasting from the internet. They weren't writing anything—everything was someone else's material.

'And that's how it's done,' Bob said, sitting back after a few minutes.

'Easy as,' Ben said.

The boys laughed.

'Some of the other groups spent weeks on this,' Bill said, shaking his head. 'And we've done it in half an hour.'

'They're all stupid,' Bob said.

Ally leaned close to her friends. 'We need to get them away from the computer,' she whispered.

'What are you doing?' asked a hushed voice from behind them. It was Jamie.

'Shhh!' Ally hissed.

Jamie ducked down next to them. The girls explained about the dead fish.

'Those guys are idiots,' Jamie agreed. 'I once heard Ben say that being triplets meant they were three times as smart as everyone else.'

'We need to get them away from the computers for a few minutes,' Ally said.

'I can help you there,' Jamie said. Without another word, he rounded the bookshelves and approached the triplets. 'Hey guys,' he said. 'The principal wants to see you.'

'What does she want?' Bill asked.

'I don't know. One of the year nines told me she wanted to see all of you immediately.'

Frowning, the boys started packing up their gear.

'Immediately,' Jamie repeated more firmly.

The boys shrugged and followed him from the library.

'Quickly!' Ally hissed.

They ran to the computers.

'What are you going to do?' Ping asked. 'Are you going to delete their work?'

'No,' Ally said. 'That would be too obvious.'

She quickly scanned the text. Their assignment was about the Second World War. There was no way they'd pass anyway. It was completely disjointed—some of the lines even finished mid-sentence.

'Someone watch the door,' Ally said. 'Tell me when they're coming.'

Ping went to the door of the library as Ally started typing.

'What are you doing?' Harmony asked.

'No time to explain,' Ally said, her eyes on the screen.

Less than five minutes later, Ping came racing back. 'They're coming! They're coming!' she squealed.

Ally quickly finished, and they hid behind the shelves. Not a moment too soon! The Tommettis headed back to the computers with Jamie in tow.

'...don't know what happened,' he was saying. 'She must have changed her mind.'

'She's old,' Ben said. 'She's probably sea lion.'

'Senile,' Jamie said.

'Whatever.'

The school bell rang.

'Quick,' Bill said. 'Print the report. History's next.'

Jamie met the girls outside the library. 'Did you really go to see the principal?' Ally asked.

'We did,' Jamie said. 'She said I must have been fooled by one of the older kids.'

The girls thanked Jamie and they all headed to class, where Mrs Brogden was waiting. A stout woman, she looked disturbingly like a frog. The kids always referred to her as Froggy Broggy behind her back.

The class began. Mrs Brogden asked Jamie's group to speak first. Bruce got up on their behalf and said they'd been researching the history of Abraham Lincoln and the civil war.

'He dies in the end,' Bill Tommetti muttered.

'Be quiet,' Mrs Brogden said.

'I saw the movie.'

'*Silence!*'

Bruce gave the report. It was well researched and Ally found it quite interesting. She'd had no idea so many people were killed. Ben Tommetti got up next to speak.

'What's your report about, Ben?' Mrs Brogden asked.

'The Second World War,' he said.

'One of history's greatest conflicts!' Mrs Brogden declared. 'Proceed!'

He began to read. 'The Second World War officially began on the ninth of September 1939, when Britain invaded Germany,' Ben said. 'The British leader at the time, Mr Frodo, had realised they needed more land. Germany's prime minister, Mr Sauron, declared war.'

Mrs Brogden's mouth fell open.

'Everyone got involved,' Ben continued. 'Even the great nation of Legolas.'

Ally glanced around. The other two Tommetti boys were sitting back in their seats, looking quite satisfied. Everyone else looked either mystified or amused.

'Captain Aragorn led the attack, with Captain Gandalf defending. It was a good thing that the supreme leader, Celeborn—'

'Silence!' Mrs Brogden roared.

Now it was time for Ben's mouth to drop open. 'What's wrong?' he asked.

'Your report! That can't be what you're handing in!'

'Why not?'

'It's...rubbish! Those are all characters from *The Lord of the Rings*!'

Now the entire class—except the Tommetti triplets—burst out laughing. Mrs Brogden ignored them.

'You might think this is funny,' she said to Ben, 'but I don't appreciate having my time wasted!'

'But...but...' Ben held up the report. 'It must be true! We copied it from the internet!'

Mrs Brogden's eyes opened wide. 'You did *what*?' she said.

# 14

**'THE WAIT** is killing me!' Ally complained.

She and her father were in the workshop, a run-down old building with a corrugated-iron roof, and years of dust smearing the windows. Tools hung from the timber walls, boxes filled with used parts packed benches around the sides, and layers of worn carpet covered the floor.

Her father was working on a small red tractor in the middle of the workshop.

'You need to learn patience,' he said. 'You remember how I wasn't very good when I first started painting? Now look at me.'

'Almost as good as Leonardo da Vinci.'

'Getting there.'

A week had passed since the girls had ordered the equipment they needed for their project. The bottle of helium, the GPS and the camera had already turned up. The fabric had also arrived, and Ping had transformed it into a bright red-and-blue parachute. They were just waiting for the balloons now, and it was driving Ally crazy.

'We're ready to make the gondola,' she said. 'But we can't do the experiments without the balloons.'

'It would be a little hard,' Russell agreed.

A bell rang out across the yard. Russell had set it up to ring when someone pressed the front door buzzer.

Russell wiped the grease off his face and cleaned his hands. 'Were you expecting anyone?' he asked as they made their way through the house.

'No. I just hope it isn't Mrs Blunt.'

It wasn't, but it was almost as bad.

'Ah,' Mr Drake said. 'You're home.' He smiled, revealing two rows of even, nicotine-stained teeth.

*No fangs*, Ally thought. *Maybe they only come out at night.* She glanced past him and saw his hearse was parked out the front.

Drake introduced himself to Russell. 'May I speak with you for a moment?' he asked.

'What's it about?' Russell asked.

'Your property,' Drake said. 'I have some interest in buying it.'

'Really? Our house?'

'Absolutely. May I come in?'

Much to Ally's consternation, Russell invited Drake inside and led the way to the living room.

'Somebody is an artist,' Drake said, looking around.

'That's me,' Russell said. 'In my spare time.'

'They're very...interesting.'

'Would you like a drink?' Russell asked.

'Water would be fine.'

Ally scampered to the kitchen. She had completely forgotten that Drake had mentioned wanting to buy their property. Her stomach was churning. This was their home! She didn't want to move!

She filled a glass and carried it back out to the living room for Drake.

'It's an old house,' the man said.

'We've lived here our whole lives,' Russell said. 'My parents bought it many years ago.'

'I only recently moved to your lovely town, but I've

grown to admire it immensely. It's a place of unlimited beauty.'

Ally had heard Yallaroo described in a lot of different ways, but 'a place of unlimited beauty' was not one of them.

'Yes,' Russell said, thoughtfully. 'It's a great place to live.'

'I've been searching for a home so I can settle here permanently. A place that would give me room to move, a clear view of the hills, and just the right ambience.'

Neither Ally nor Russell said anything.

'My search has brought me here,' Drake said. 'Your home—it's an excellent example of early twentieth-century grandeur.'

'Thank you,' Russell said.

Drake sniffed. 'Clearly it needs restoration,' he said. 'New plumbing, a new roof, new paint—'

'I'm sorry,' Russell said. 'But we're not interested in selling.'

Drake smiled tightly. 'Everyone says that,' he said. 'But everyone has a price.'

'We don't want to sell. I have my business here, and—'

'You can move your business elsewhere.'

'That would take a lot of work. Besides, as I said, we've lived here our whole lives. We're happy here and have no reason to sell.'

'Surely it's a matter of price.'

'It's not.'

'Every property is for sale at the right price,' Drake said. 'Imagine what you could do with the money. Build a nice, new home closer to town. Even move to a different town entirely. Leave this drab little place behind.'

'I thought you said Yallaroo had unlimited beauty.'

Drake paused. 'Beauty is in the eye of the beholder,' he said.

'Anyway,' Russell said, 'we have no interest in selling. There are lots of other houses in the area—'

'What's your price?'

'There is no price. We're not selling.'

'Name a number.'

'I'm sorry,' Russell said, starting to stand, 'but we're busy right now. Thanks for dropping by—'

'Just give me a number and we can work it out.'

Russell took a deep breath. 'There is no number,' he said firmly. 'There is no price. I'll show you out.'

Drake didn't move. For a moment, he looked like he was about to lose his temper, but then he smiled a nasty smile. 'You've been most kind,' he said, standing. 'Thank you for taking the time to speak with me.'

They silently showed Drake to the front door, and he drove off in his hearse. Ally and Russell watched it disappear from sight.

'Strange,' Russell said. 'Very strange.'

# 15

**'OKAY,' ALLY** said. 'Now for the next step.'

The girls were in her bedroom with all their equipment arranged on her bed. The three balloons had finally arrived.

What really surprised Ally was the size of the balloons. She'd expected them to be enormous, but uninflated, they were barely half her height.

'I've been thinking about the gondola,' Ping said. 'It's going to have to be as light as possible. It has to hold the camera, the GPS and anything else that we send up.'

'What else would we send?' Harmony asked.

'I'd like to send Barbie.'

'Huh?'

'That's how we first met!' Ping said. 'You remember our first day of school? We all brought Barbie dolls to school?'

'I remember,' Harmony said. 'I burnt mine in a sacrificial bonfire because I decided that Barbie was an unrealistic representation of womanhood.'

'And you were right,' Ally said. 'I read somewhere that her proportions are all wrong. Her waist is impossibly thin, her legs are too long, and her hands and feet are too small. If she were a real person, she wouldn't be able to stand up.' She paused. 'Still, she's a symbol of where we were and where we can go. She's been an astronaut, a doctor, an architect, heaps of things.'

Harmony sighed. 'Let me think about it,' she said.

They set to work on the gondola.

At first Ally had thought about making something that looked like a spaceship. Then she remembered that Russell had pointed out that they needed to keep the weight down.

'The lighter the gondola,' he'd said, 'the higher the balloon will travel.'

What they'd decided to do was build an open-sided

triangular pyramid. The camera and GPS would be open to the elements, but that would be okay as long as the parachute worked correctly. From the top of the pyramid would run a short length of rope which would pass through the middle of the parachute and up to the balloon.

Ally produced several short lengths of balsa wood. 'People use it to make model aeroplanes, because it's so light. Dad had some lying around his workshop. We can cut it to shape and then bolt the pieces together.'

They tried bracing a piece of the wood against the top of Ally's desk, but it wouldn't hold still while they sawed.

'Your dad has all sorts of stuff in his workshop,' Ping said. 'Maybe he can help.'

Ally felt like kicking herself. 'You're right,' she said. 'He's got everything we need.'

They went down to the workshop, where they found Russell working on a rusty engine. He examined the timber.

'Use a vice to secure it,' he said. 'Once you've cut the pieces to size, you can drill holes through the ends so bolts will slide through. Maybe use glue as well as bolts when you're joining the pieces of wood together.' He paused. 'I can make it if you want.'

Ally chewed her lip. 'It's okay,' she said. 'It's our project. We need to do the work.'

Russell smiled. 'Good on you,' he said, and pointed them to a nearby workbench.

Ally tightened one of the pieces in the vice—and immediately broke it.

'I think that was too tight,' Ping said.

'Good thing we've got plenty of wood,' Ally said.

'Let me do the cutting,' Harmony said. 'I'm good with tools.'

She was. After cutting the wood without difficulty, Harmony used a hand drill to make fine holes through the timber. Ally and Ping marvelled at her handiwork as she assembled the pyramid. Soon she had the whole thing glued and bolted together.

Harmony frowned. 'There's something I'm still unclear about,' she said. 'How does the parachute unfold?'

'It's not like a typical parachute that people use when they jump out of a plane,' Ping explained. 'This parachute is located directly under the balloon. When the balloon pops, the gondola will fall, and the drag of the air causes the parachute to open.'

When they were sure the glue was completely dry, they lifted the gondola experimentally.

'It's *really* light,' Harmony said.

'We still need to attach the GPS,' Ally said. 'And the camera.'

'And work out the dates for the launches,' Ping said.

They checked the calendars on their phones. The term was passing all too quickly. Study for end-of-year exams had already begun, and the closing date for the contest was only a few weeks away.

'We can do our first launch next Saturday,' Ally suggested. 'We could do the next one a week later, and the third one the week after that.'

'That doesn't leave us a lot of time to submit our final results,' Ping said.

'We'll get in just in time,' Ally said. 'We can't leave it any later.'

Russell ambled over to see how they were going.

'That's a *very* neat rig,' he said, glancing at his watch. 'Now, does anyone feel like one of my famous hot chocolates?'

No one said no.

**'THOSE BOYS** are plotting,' Harmony said. 'And I don't like it.'

The girls were in the quadrangle, keeping an eye on the Tommetti triplets on the opposite side. The boys had their heads huddled together.

'Do you think they know we sabotaged their presentation?' Harmony asked.

'Maybe,' Ping said. 'Maybe not.'

'I'm sure they do,' Ally said. 'Bill Tommetti glared at me yesterday.'

'We can arrange a horrible accident for them if we need to,' Harmony said. 'I still have access to dynamite. I can even track down a tarantula if you give me enough time.'

Ally sighed. 'We need to forget about them,' she said, 'and focus on our project.'

They had to deliver a short report in Miss Kapoor's class in ten minutes about their progress.

The bell rang.

'We'll be fine,' Harmony said. 'Let's go.'

Miss Kapoor was already waiting for them. The Tommetti triplets presented first. The boys took turns, describing how they had done a lot of research in the library and on the internet, and how they were almost certain that lizard people were around today.

'What's your evidence for this?' Miss Kapoor asked.

'We have pictures,' Ben said. He pulled a photocopy from a folder and showed it to the class. The picture showed a woman wearing a human mask that had been ripped in half. Beneath it lay a reptile face. 'This is clear proof that lizard people walk among us.'

The Tommetti triplets nodded confidently.

Miss Kapoor stared at the image. 'That's from a movie called *Attack of the Reptilians*,' she said.

'Huh?' Ben said.

'It's a movie. I saw it when it first came out.' She shook her head. 'Terrible film.'

'But...but...'

'And your other "evidence"?'

'Well...er...' Reaching into his folder, Ben found another image and held it up to show the class. 'Here!'

'That's a Gorn from *Star Trek*.'

'The...'

'It's a Gorn,' Miss Kapoor informed him. 'A member of an alien race that Captain Kirk fights.'

'Okay.' Back to the folder. 'And these?'

'The Silurians from *Doctor Who*. One of the more interesting alien races to appear in the series.'

Now the Tommetti triplets were completely lost for words. Miss Kapoor told them to sit down.

'You recall I said that you needed real evidence?' she said. 'That means *actual* real evidence. Not pictures downloaded from the internet.'

'But—'

'I'll talk to you all after class.' Miss Kapoor turned to Jamie and his team. 'Who's speaking for the Busy Bees?'

'I am,' Charlotte said. She'd brought a laptop in

with her. After setting it up, she went through a slide display. 'We've planted flowers at different locations around Yallaroo,' she said. 'Around half of them are Australian natives. The other half are European.' She changed to an image of a camera. 'At first we had problems counting the bees. Now we have cameras set up with motion detectors. They take a photo every time a bee passes by the sensor.'

Miss Kapoor asked them a few questions about their project. 'Well done,' she said. 'Now let's find out how the Balloon Girls are faring.'

The Tommetti triplets tittered at the back of the room. Miss Kapoor gave them a stern look as Ally got up to give their report.

She explained that they'd received their supplies and had constructed the gondola for the balloon. 'We're launching our first flight this Saturday,' she said. 'I've verified the flight details with the Civil Aviation Safety Authority.'

'Where are you launching from?' Miss Kapoor asked.

'The Mitchell farm,' Ally said. 'It's off Dry River Road.'

Her father had been able to arrange a launching

place with the Mitchell family. They were local sheep farmers.

'That's very exciting,' Miss Kapoor said.

The class ended, everyone packed their bags and headed for the bus stop. Ally and the others were chatting when she realised that Jamie was hovering at her elbow. She smiled at him.

'Hey,' he said, trying to sound casual. 'Got a minute?'

'Uh, sure,' she said.

He motioned towards one of the demountables. Ally dropped her bag and followed him. The other girls stopped and stared as she looked back at them over her shoulder.

'*What's going on?*' Harmony mouthed.

Ally frowned. '*Go away!*' she mouthed back.

It was quiet behind the demountable, but hot. The late-afternoon sun beat down with a vengeance, and the fields and hills behind the school were brown and dry. Summer had come early, and the countryside desperately needed a downpour.

'Er,' Jamie began. 'How have you been?'

'Great. Probably about the same as I was five minutes ago in class.'

'Yeah. Me too.'

Neither of them said anything. Ally looked past Jamie. Peeping around the corner were Ping and Harmony. They were making *kissy-kissy* faces!

Ally ignored them and looked back at Jamie.

'You know the Twilight Movie nights are starting from next Friday,' he said. 'The first movie is *The Wizard of Oz*.'

'I saw that when I was younger,' Ally said. 'It's a nice movie.'

'Would you like to go?' Jamie asked.

She was just about to reply that she'd rather see a sci-fi film when she realised that Jamie was asking if she wanted to go with him. Her with him. The two of them together.

A date.

'My mum can take us,' he added.

*Oh dear*, she thought. *I wasn't expecting this*.

She didn't want to hurt his feelings. He seemed nice, but she didn't want to give him the wrong idea.

'That sounds fine,' she said. 'Except...'

'What?'

Ally swallowed hard, and realised her face was turning red. 'I don't want you to think...I mean... I just want us to be friends.'

She found herself staring at the ground as she said this. When she looked up, she could see hurt in his eyes. 'I'm sorry,' she said.

'That's okay.' He swallowed hard. 'We'll just go as friends.'

'Great. It would be interesting to see that film.'

She glanced past Jamie to see Harmony and Ping doing a little happy dance on the spot. Ally rolled her eyes.

'Are you okay?' Jamie asked.

She gestured helplessly at her friends.

Jamie turned and saw them mid-step. 'Yeah,' he said. 'There's no cure for that.'

As they all started back to the school buses, Ping glanced about. 'Where are our bags?' she asked.

The Tommetti triplets were sitting on a bench nearby, laughing hysterically, and pointing at one of the departing school buses. Something had been tied to the back of the bus and was being dragged down the street.

Their bags!

**THE WEEKEND** arrived all too quickly. The night before the flight, Ally and the others realised they had logged the test flight with CASA but hadn't checked the latest weather report. They hadn't written anything about their expected results, either. They gathered at Ping's place and put together all their paperwork, and checked the weather.

'It's supposed to be a fine day,' Harmony said, reading her phone.

'You mean hot,' Ally said. 'The same as every other day.'

'As long as the weather's fine tomorrow,' Ping said.

'That's all I care about.'

They turned up at the Mitchells' farm a little after eight o'clock, and the sky was clear as predicted. To Ally's surprise, there was a small group waiting. Harmony's mum and Ping's parents were there. So were Mrs Mitchell and her three kids. Jamie and his mum had also turned up—he was going to video the launch.

But the biggest surprise was Miss Kapoor.

'Hello, miss,' Ally said, smiling.

The teacher greeted the girls and their parents, stopping at Russell. 'And you must be Ally's father,' she said.

'So glad you could make it,' Russell said, wringing her hand. 'You've been such an inspiration to the girls.'

'Happy to be of help,' Miss Kapoor said. 'We all need to dream big.'

'That's what I always say.'

Ally wasn't sure she'd ever heard her dad say that, but this was no time to mention it. They had a lot of work to do. Russell suggested cordoning off the area so Ally and the others had room to work. It was a good idea.

They arranged all their equipment: helium bottle,

balloon, gondola, rope and parachute.

'That's really well made,' Miss Kapoor said, admiring the gondola and the parachute. 'Who sewed the parachute?'

'I did,' Ping said.

'She's very good with a needle,' Mrs Chong said. 'She'll be a surgeon one day.'

Ping turned and mouthed '*No way!*' at Ally and Harmony.

Jamie had come with his mum, Laura. He wanted to film the launch on his phone.

'Is this okay?' he asked Ally. He wanted to upload the footage to a website he'd made. 'It might be a good way to promote your project.'

'Uh, sure,' she said, feeling a bit overwhelmed by all the attention. 'Just make certain you get our good sides.'

'I'll do my best.'

As well as filming the girls, he started interviewing people in the crowd.

'I hope this works,' Harmony murmured.

'It better,' Ping said. 'Otherwise we're going to look a bit silly.'

The girls attached the camera to the gondola and

began filming before attaching the GPS. Ally started up the laptop.

After a moment, she gave a yell. 'We're picking up the signal!' she said.

The screen showed a map of the area with a tiny red dot in the middle.

'That's the GPS,' Ally said, pointing.

They attached the rope to the gondola and ran the other end through the parachute. This end would attach to the balloon.

'Now we just need to blow up the balloon,' Ally said.

She attached the nozzle to the helium bottle. There was a slight hiss as the balloon rapidly started to inflate. Harmony held the balloon steady until it was over a metre across. The helium was driving it upright against the force of gravity.

Finally, when the balloon was about as big as a person, they tied off the nozzle and connected the rope.

A slight breeze tugged at the balloon as they lifted it high. Ping and Harmony held onto it as Ally double-checked that the signal was still coming through.

'Perfect,' she said. 'Okay, the time is eight twenty-seven am, and the wind speed is four knots. I'm just going to make a record of that.' She looked back at the screen. 'The wind's coming from the south-east, and the temperature is sixteen degrees Celsius.' She made a note of those numbers too.

'Are we ready?' she asked.

'Yep,' Ping said. 'Good to go.'

Ally swallowed. A lot was depending on this. They would be flying off to the US if the project were a success.

'Let's do it,' Harmony said.

They released the balloon. It soared upwards like a bird released from captivity, as if it wanted nothing more than to get as high and as far away from the Earth as possible.

The small crowd burst into applause as it raced into the sky.

'Wow,' Ally said, transfixed by the sight. 'Wow.'

Everyone grouped around them. Hugs and handshakes were exchanged all round. Ally returned to the laptop.

'The balloon's 860 metres above sea level,' she said, 'and it's drifting north-west at a speed of five knots.'

The balloon had already become a small white dot in the sky. Ally glanced down at the laptop. When she looked back up again, it had disappeared from sight.

Ping examined the laptop, leaning in to see the numbers ticking over on the screen. 'It's rising steadily, at about six metres per second,' she said. 'It's just over a kilometre high now.'

They moved the laptop to the bonnet of the nearest car so everyone could watch the numbers as the balloon soared higher and higher: two kilometres, three kilometres, four kilometres.

Miss Kapoor pointed at the screen. 'It's moving to the north-west. It's about two kilometres from where we are now.'

'We'd better get moving,' Russell said. 'We need to be nearby when it lands.'

The Mitchells had to stay at their farm, but everyone else piled into their respective cars, with the girls crowding the back seat of Russell's dual-cab ute. The girls pored over the laptop as they started off in pursuit.

'It's angling further north now,' Harmony said.

Ally glanced behind. A convoy of cars was following; everyone wanted to see this through to the end.

They spent the next couple of hours bouncing over hills and along dusty roads. At first they headed towards Cobram, but soon the GPS steered them east in the direction of the tiny town of Glenrowan, where bushranger Ned Kelly had famously donned his makeshift suit of armour to go into battle against the police—and lost.

A farmer driving his tractor sedately down a country road stopped and stared.

*He's never seen so many cars on this road at once*, Ally thought.

It was impossible to guess where the balloon would land.

Harmony gave an excited cry. 'It's stopped moving,' she said. 'Wait! It's falling!'

'The balloon's burst!' Ping said.

'It reached its maximum height,' Ally said, studying the screen. 'It reached thirty-four thousand, six hundred and two metres above sea level. Now we've just got to find where it lands.'

They tracked the signal to a property outside of Chesney Vale. There were no houses there. No shops. Just a few scraggly eucalyptus trees lining the road against a backdrop of dull, husk-coloured fields and undulating hills.

Russell pulled over, and they all climbed out. As they sat the laptop on the bonnet again, everyone else piled out of their cars and gathered round to read the screen.

'It's not far away,' Ally said, examining the map closely. She glanced around to get her bearings. 'It's that way,' she said. 'East.'

'We can't just go swarming over someone's property,' Russell said. 'It's trespassing.'

They soon found a letterbox, and a dirt-covered driveway leading to a house hidden behind a nearby hill. Jamie's mum, Laura, offered to speak to the owner.

She drove up to the house and returned a few minutes later. 'Good news,' she said. 'The owner's a nice old man, and he said it's fine for us to search his land.'

It took less than an hour to find the gondola. It was still in one piece—Ping's parachute had worked perfectly.

Ally removed the camera from the gondola. 'The camera looks fine,' she said. 'I can hardly wait to see the footage.'

**ALLY AND** the girls returned to her place to view the footage. They grouped around the gondola in Ally's room as Harmony carefully removed the memory card from the camera.

'I've never seen a memory card like this before,' she said. 'Where did you get it?'

'Dad had a bunch of these lying in a drawer,' Ally said.

They inserted the card into a slot on Ally's laptop. Ally double-clicked on the movie file and it started to play.

'That's us!' Ping squealed.

The image briefly captured glimpses of them before reeling about to show the sky. Then it wheeled downwards again to show a closeup of brown grass and dozens of pairs of feet as the gondola was placed onto the ground. A few minutes passed as the balloon was inflated. A shoe blocked the view of the camera.

'That's my shoe,' Harmony said.

'It needs a clean,' Ping said.

'Now you're sounding like your mother.'

'Forget I said anything.'

They heard Harmony's voice as they prepared to release the balloon.

*'Let's do it,'* she said.

The image shifted sharply and they saw a flash of the crowd, the field—and then nothing as the screen went blank. The girls stared at the dark screen.

'What's going on?' Ping asked.

'I don't know,' Ally said.

She felt a sinking feeling in her stomach as she started the file again. It played perfectly, showing the same piece of footage before dying once more.

'What's wrong?' Harmony asked. 'Is it broken?'

'I...don't know,' Ally said. 'It seems okay.'

At that moment, Russell appeared in the doorway. 'How's it going?' he asked.

The girls explained what was happening, and Russell sat down at Ally's laptop. He examined the video. 'Hmm,' he said. 'The file seems okay. I think the problem is the size of the card.'

'The card?' Ally said.

'Where did you get it from?'

'One of the drawers in the lounge room.'

'Oh dear.'

'What? What's wrong?'

He examined the file properties. 'This is an old memory card,' he said. 'It's working fine, but these old memory cards don't store very much. They're fine to hold a few photos, but video takes up far more memory, especially if it's being shot at high-definition.'

Ally felt sick. She had deliberately switched the camera to high-definition mode. She'd wanted to make certain they captured the best quality footage possible.

'So...it hasn't worked,' she said in a small voice.

'You need a bigger capacity memory card,' Russell explained. 'You can probably afford to shoot at a slightly lower resolution too. That'll extend your recording time.'

Ally felt like bursting into tears. Their efforts had been wasted, and it was all her fault. Russell explained it was easy to find larger capacity cards.

'Don't be too disappointed,' Russell said to the girls. 'You're conducting an experiment, after all, and learning is part of the process.'

He left them, offering to make some of his famous hot chocolates.

'It's my fault,' Ally said. 'I'm sorry.'

'It's not your fault,' Harmony said. 'We're all responsible for everything that happens. We've still got plenty of money left from car washing. We can easily buy a larger capacity memory card for the camera.'

'And your dad was right,' Ping added. 'This whole thing is an experiment. We can't expect everything to go smoothly.'

♣

Winston was barking.

Ally groaned. She blearily opened her eyes and read the clock. Two in the morning.

'Go back to sleep,' she groaned.

The little dachshund kept barking. Snapping her

light on, Ally saw him standing by the door, looking at her expectantly.

'What is it?' she said. 'Is someone outside?'

Ally followed Winston into the hallway—and bumped into her father. He was dressed in his pyjamas and carrying a cricket bat.

'Do you think it's a burglar?' Ally asked.

'No,' he said. 'I just felt like a game of cricket.'

They hurried to the back door, and Winston went charging outside.

'You wait here,' Russell told Ally.

'Are you kidding?'

She snatched up a metal pipe from near the back door and followed him.

A cold wind had come up. Clouds scudded across the moonlit sky as a loose piece of iron banged in the breeze. Ally's eyes swept the horizon. Distant trees swayed in the night. The blades of a half-collapsed windmill spun silently.

Winston barked, and they followed him through the yard.

A sound came from behind some broken farm machinery. 'Who's there?' Russell demanded, and a rabbit went bounding into the darkness.

They spent another half-hour searching, but the work yard was empty. Reaching the open back door, Ally was about to go back inside when Russell grabbed her arm.

'Didn't we close that?' he asked.

They had.

'It could have blown open,' Ally suggested.

'Not likely.'

Russell raised the cricket bat as they entered. They conducted a thorough search of the house from top to bottom but found nothing. If anyone had been inside, they were long gone.

Ally peeked out through the front window and saw the rear lights of a car disappearing behind the hill.

'Could it be Drake?' she asked.

'I don't know why,' Russell said. 'It seems unlikely that he'd break into our house. Unless he really wanted one of my paintings...'

They went back to bed, but Ally was up again early the next morning. She needed to know why Drake—or someone else—was so interested in their house. This meant she had to do some research.

Searching the internet revealed little. It was Sunday, but fortunately the library was open for half a day, so she decided to go there to find out what she could. Samantha, the librarian, pointed her towards the local history section.

'Everything we have on the town is back here,' she said, revealing a room not much bigger than a wardrobe. All it contained was a desk, a chair and a single wall of books.

'A few short histories were published about twenty years ago,' Samantha said, pointing to some volumes stacked on the desk. 'The shelves are mostly back issues of the *Yallaroo Weekly*. They provide the best information.'

The *Yallaroo Weekly* had been the town newspaper, but it had shut down ten years before.

'Were you after anything in particular?' Samantha asked. 'Is it Hicky Saw? That's usually what gets people interested in the history of the town.'

'Hicky Saw's real?'

'Absolutely. Check out the issues from 1914.'

She left Ally to her research.

Ally began by going through the town ledger. It was a handwritten book with details of every building in the town. Ally's house was listed as being built by William Smith in 1904, and her dad's workshop had begun life as a shed. Mrs Blunt's house had been built at the same time by Smith to house his two elderly aunts. After their deaths, the land was subdivided, and her building sold off to someone by the name of Tillerman.

Checking the 1911 census records, Ally discovered that Smith had been a local sheep farmer. His wife's name was Maureen, and their children were Rose and Lily.

Looking through one of the local history books, Ally was amazed to find a picture of her home with Mrs Blunt's house next door.

'Wow,' Ally said.

Their properties had once been new, spick and span. The shed at the back of their home looked small; someone must have built on to make it a workshop.

After that she turned her attention to the old newspapers, wondering if she might find some mention of William Smith and his family. To her surprise, the old newspapers were fascinating, and she was soon engrossed. Ally almost forgot what she'd come to the library for until Samantha came to remind her that they'd be closing in half an hour.

She started skimming through the newspapers,

but when Ally reached the latter months of 1914, what she read stunned her. She was still sitting there staring blankly at the page in front of her, her head whirling, when Samantha came to shoo her out into the late-afternoon light.

Sitting outside the library, she quickly made a call to Harmony and Ping.

'Okay,' she said. 'You're not going to believe this. Hicky Saw was a real person.'

'Only if you think of a monster as a person,' Ping said.

'He saws off people's arms and legs,' Harmony added.

Ally sighed. 'Maybe,' she said. 'But I don't think so. He was a bank robber who lived about a hundred years ago.'

'A bank robber?' Ping said.

'The police eventually tracked him to Yallaroo. He had a shootout with police in 1914 but escaped. The police thought he might have been injured, but he was never captured or seen again.' She paused. 'And the shootout happened on our street!'

'Seriously?' Harmony said. 'So he might literally have crawled under your house and died.'

'It's impossible to get under our house,' Ally said. 'I've tried. But get this—the police never found the treasure!'

'Treasure?' Ping said. 'What treasure?'

'All the money from his robberies!' Ally said. 'None of it was ever recovered. It was probably a fortune!'

'That's amazing!' Harmony said. 'Drake must be after the treasure and thinks it's in your house.'

Ally sighed. 'I would have noticed if it were lying around,' she said. 'And Dad's repaired just about every inch of the building, and he's never found anything.' She shook her head forlornly. 'Drake, or someone else, thinks the treasure is in our home, but they're wrong!'

# 19

**ALLY WAS** busy the next week studying, finishing assignments and planning the second balloon's flight. She went out and bought a new memory card for the camera. This one had a much higher capacity and could record for hours. By the time Friday arrived, she'd almost forgotten about agreeing to go to the movies with Jamie.

'You're still okay for tonight?' he asked her at lunchtime on Friday. 'I know you've got the second flight tomorrow.'

'Yes, it's fine,' Ally said, still concerned about giving him the wrong impression. 'Going to the movie will be fun.'

'We'll pick you up around eight o'clock if that's all right.'

'Great.'

The next struggle was working out what to wear. When she arrived home, she eventually decided on a pair of jeans and a new t-shirt she'd bought. It had a quote on the front: *Genius is 1% inspiration and 99% perspiration*. When she rang Ping and Harmony, they were less than enthusiastic about it.

'What about a dress instead?' Ping suggested.

'I don't think I own one.'

'Could you make a dress?' Harmony asked.

'Make a dress?' Ally's head spun. 'From what? Paper mâché?'

Ally said goodnight and joined her father in the kitchen.

'You look nice,' he said.

'Thanks,' she said, glancing around. Jamie's family ran cattle on a hundred acres on a property a few kilometres out from the other side of town. She'd never been to their house, but she knew it was large and modern with a nice garden.

'What is it?' Russell asked.

Ally didn't quite know what to say. 'Our house,' she said. 'It's a bit...run-down.'

Russell glanced about. 'It's *very* run-down,' he said. 'Are you worried about what Jamie and his mum will think?'

'Sort of.'

'Jamie's parents are the same as us,' Russell said. 'They're working people just doing their best.' He glanced around. 'But I promise we'll repaint when we get a chance.'

There was a knock at the front door.

'That's them,' Ally said.

'Relax,' Russell advised.

He opened the front door to reveal Jamie and Laura. To Ally's relief, Laura greeted her father on the doorstep, beckoned at Ally to come out, and then headed straight off before Russell could invite them in.

The area around the old jam factory was busy. The projector had been erected on the back of a truck and was already showing old black-and-white cartoons. People were setting up deckchairs and picnic blankets. An ice-cream van was doing a roaring trade. Kids were running around everywhere.

The sun had already disappeared behind the hills,

leaving only a curtain of light and, above it, a sheet of blinking stars. Laura arranged their deckchairs before heading off to buy ice creams.

'I was worried you might not come out tonight,' Jamie said.

'Why?'

'I thought you might have become "inflated" by your own importance.'

'Jamie, that's the worst joke I've ever heard.'

'It was pretty bad.'

'Besides, our first experiment was a complete failure.' She'd told Miss Kapoor and the class what had happened to their recording. Everyone had been sympathetic, except for the Tommetti triplets who had burst out laughing. 'I'll feel better once tomorrow's over.'

'A lot of the town is interested. Some people at Moo Moo's were talking about it the other day.'

'Really?'

'And I've loaded my first video onto the website.'

'What video?'

'You remember the filming I did the other day?'

Ally nodded. She'd forgotten that Jamie had said he'd upload it.

'It's already getting a few hits. It's not every day that someone launches a weather balloon.'

'Actually,' Ally said, 'they probably *do* get launched every day.'

'But not in Yallaroo.'

'That's true.' She thought for a moment. 'Anyway,' she said, 'how's your project going?'

Jamie rubbed his chin. 'We're collecting information,' he said. 'It's not very exciting. A lot of it is just adding up numbers. The hardest thing has been keeping the plants alive.'

'Because of the drought?'

It still hadn't rained. A cold change was coming through, but no rain was expected.

'We've had to water them by hand every day, but we made the mistake of planting them a long way from any taps. We have to walk almost a kilometre.'

'Wow.'

Laura arrived back at that moment with the ice creams. The movie started, and Ally settled back to enjoy it. The film was better than she remembered. She'd completely forgotten the wizard didn't have any real magical powers.

'I'd forgotten that too,' Laura said.

'He was just a conman,' Jamie said.

'There's plenty of those around,' Ally said. 'Some flat earthers make their money by publishing books or through advertising attached to their videos on the net. It's just a big scam.'

Arriving at her place, Ally said goodnight to Jamie and Laura and headed inside. She told her dad she'd had a nice evening, headed for her room, and got ready for bed. Ally hadn't checked her phone all night and found that Harmony and Ping had both left her a dozen messages. She glanced through them. *Have you done any kissing? Is he a good kisser? Has he declared his eternal love for you?*

Ally rolled her eyes.

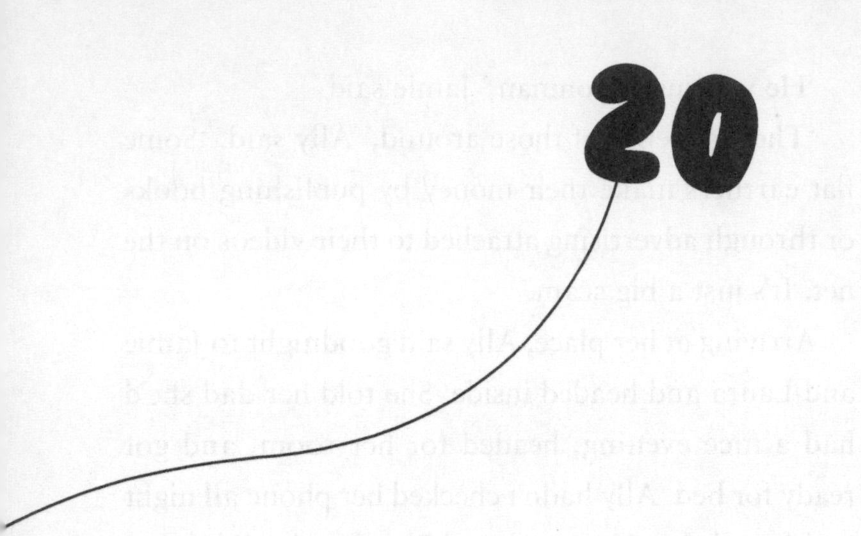


**THE ALARM** went off the next morning, but Ally was already out of bed. She had showered and was almost ready to head out the door when her father cornered her.

'Have you looked outside?' he asked.

'What do you mean?'

She peered out the window. This was more than a cold change. It was almost a gale. Churning clouds filled the morning sky, brown dust shrouded the distant hills, and trees were blowing around wildly.

'Hey,' she said. 'That's windy.'

'It'll be fine,' Russell assured her. 'We'll just have to be careful.'

They loaded their supplies into the ute, headed off and reached the launch site in good time. Much to Ally's surprise, there were more than fifty people waiting.

'What's going on?' Ally asked.

'They're here to see the launch,' Harmony said.

'What?'

'Word's got around,' Ping said. 'This is the biggest thing Yallaroo has ever seen.' She stopped. 'Except for the time the old chemist shop caught fire. Or maybe when Robbie Smith's snake collection got loose. Or when—'

They laid out their equipment on the ground. Miss Kapoor was there, as were Jamie and his mum. Jamie filmed as Laura kept the small crowd out of the girls' way.

The wind picked up again and sent the gondola end over end across the dry grass. Ping retrieved it, then they attached the GPS and camera. They started the camera and saw on its display that it had more than two hours of recording time. Then they checked the line leading to the parachute. It was fine. Ally confirmed that the connection between the GPS and laptop were working too as Ping and Harmony started to inflate the balloon.

'Hold tight,' Harmony said, as the wind threatened to rip it from their grasp.

'But not too tight,' Ping said. 'We don't want to burst it by accident.'

Russell and Mrs Mitchell stepped forward to help brace the balloon. It was getting bigger by the second. Soon it was the height of a small person. Ally's heart was pounding. If they released the balloon by accident, it would be away in an instant, and probably be punctured by a nearby tree or fence.

They gave it a few more seconds.

'That's it,' Harmony said, and they tied off the neck.

'I'll attach the rope to the balloon,' Ally said. She did this and gripped the rope tightly. 'Now lift the balloon up higher.'

Everyone did as requested as Ally slowly let the rope run between her fingers, and she gripped the gondola. The balloon bobbed about wildly, torn between wanting to soar upwards or career sideways into the tree line.

‘We need to launch!’ Ping yelled above the roar of the wind.

Ally nodded. ‘Okay,’ she said. ‘On the count of three. One...two...three!’

The balloon leapt upwards, taking the gondola with it. People started clapping, and Ally let out a sigh of relief.

Russell gave her a hug. ‘Well done,’ he said.

‘Let’s hope we have better luck this time,’ Ally said.

The balloon was already high above them and leaping away to the north. Ping was watching the signal on the laptop.

‘The balloon’s moving fast,’ she yelled. ‘It’s at twenty-four knots.’

‘We’d better go,’ Russell said.

The convoy of vehicles was bigger this time. It was like a car rally as Russell’s car, with Ally and the others in the back seat, went barrelling down the road after the balloon. The wind seemed stronger than ever. The whole landscape was obliterated by red dust. Trees were being tossed about as if in a washing machine.

*We should have postponed*, Ally thought. *Doing anything in this weather is dangerous.*

She studied the laptop. The tiny red dot seemed to be charging across the map.

'It's already four kilometres east of us,' Ping said.

'Height is at two thousand metres,' Harmony said. 'It's still rising but being pushed east.'

Ally looked up. The sky was a messy mash of dark clouds. She imagined their balloon navigating its way through a stormy channel of airborne reefs and shoals.

*What if it rains?*

But it wouldn't rain, though they desperately needed it. Days and weeks of it, really.

They drove on.

The angry wind tossed the eucalypts and wattles, sending leaves and shards of bark skidding across the road. White cockatoos scattered haphazardly into the sky. A mob of kangaroos went racing through a paddock and disappeared into the dust storm.

A man was walking down one of the country roads. He stared at the convoy in surprise before being swallowed up by a sea of dust.

The wind kept pushing the balloon to the east. Russell kept pace, skirting towns large and small. Baddaginnie. Winton. Myrtleford. It seemed the journey would never end. Ally glanced back and saw that some of the cars had given up. They'd obviously decided the cross-country dash was too dangerous.

A few diehards continued to follow, however, including Jamie and his mother, and Miss Kapoor.

'The balloon's height is just over thirty-five thousand metres,' Ping said. 'Oh!'

'It's burst,' Harmony said. 'And falling.'

They were right. The balloon was dropping rapidly.

'It's coming down near Mongans Bridge,' Ally said.

'That's in the high country,' Russell added. 'It'll take us a while to get there. You might want to tell the others.'

Ally and the girls rang the other people in the convoy, but they were still keen. Another hour passed before they reached the area. Despite having lived in Yallaroo all her life, Ally had rarely visited this region at the foot of the Victorian Alps.

Bush-covered hills bordered both sides of a long, narrow valley. The farms were a mix of sheep stations, hobby farms and vineyards. A few small wineries and restaurants nestled amongst the acres of squat grapevines. The vines were green and lush at this time of year.

'Slow down,' Ally instructed. 'We're getting close.'

At least the wind had died down. Soon they were pulling over to the side of the road. Climbing out, Ally and the girls examined the laptop as other cars stopped and about twenty people squeezed around them.

'I think it's come down in a vineyard,' Ping said.

'I think you're right,' Ally said, pointing. 'It's out there somewhere.'

Acres of grapevines blanketed the landscape.

'It could take hours to find,' Harmony said.

'Oh no!' Ping cried.

'What is it?' Ally asked.

Ping pointed wordlessly.

A small dam sat behind a building nestled among the fields. Square in the middle of the dam floated a familiar red and blue parachute.

'It's landed in the water!' Harmony said. 'We've got to get it out.'

'Wait here,' Russell said. 'We can't have everyone charging onto this person's property.'

He hurried up the driveway, and they watched him converse with a couple at the front door. Then he traipsed off around the side of the house with them to the dam. They watched as he waded into the water to retrieve the soggy payload.

He returned a few minutes later, grim faced. 'It's not looking good,' he said. 'The gondola was upside down in the water.'

The girls gingerly examined the apparatus. Ally disconnected the camera, opened it up, and water poured out.

'Oh no,' she said. 'This is wrecked.'

Miss Kapoor stepped forward. 'The memory card might still be all right,' she said. 'I have a friend who's a photographer. He'll know.'

Ally nodded. There seemed to be little else that could be done.

# 

**MISS KAPOOR** rang Ally early the next morning about the memory card, but the news was bad.

'He did everything he could to retrieve the information,' she said. 'But it looks like the file's completely corrupted.'

'All right,' Ally said, her throat catching. This was the second time that things had gone wrong.

'Don't take it too hard,' Miss Kapoor said. 'All experimentation involves ups and downs, and your project is no different.'

'Thanks, miss,' Ally said.

She hung up and rang Harmony and Ping. They

were disappointed, but not surprised at the news.

'This means we should probably change the design of the gondola,' Ping said. 'Maybe build a new one.'

'I can do that,' Harmony offered. 'I've got an idea about something that might work.'

'The GPS has also stopped working,' Ally said. She'd taken everything back to her place after the landing. 'We'll need to buy a new one.'

'As well as a camera and memory card,' Harmony said.

Ally made some quick calculations. 'We made plenty of money from the car wash,' she said. 'We still have enough to buy everything we need.'

'At least the parachute is fine,' Ping said. 'And at least we don't need to buy a new balloon.'

'I know. That took weeks.'

The girls purchased the replacement equipment online. They spent all of Sunday working on their report, but Ping was the one who excelled at making it look good. She entered all the information into a spreadsheet and created graphs that showed the balloon's rate of ascent and distance travelled over time. It was a shame there was no footage from the camera, but it was important to keep a record of everything that had occurred anyway.

Ally couldn't stop herself from thinking about the Smithsonian. There were so many exciting things there. It was in Washington, so they could do a tour of the city's historic buildings while they were there too.

*We're sure to win just as long as we have some video footage,* she thought. *The third flight has got to be successful!*

☁

Ally spent the remainder of the day working on some maths homework while Russell repaired a tractor engine. They were both too tired to make dinner, so he suggested they go out.

'Moo Moo's?' he said.

'Is there anywhere else?'

'Only if you want to drive to Benalla.'

'Moo Moo's it is.'

After Ally spent a few hours on some homework, they jumped in the ute and made their way to the café. Much to Ally's surprise, they found Miss Kapoor sitting in a seat near the window.

'Hello, miss,' Ally said.

'Oh, hello,' the teacher said, smiling. She had been reading a book. 'Come for dinner?'

'We have,' Russell said. 'Would you like to join us?'

'I don't want to impose—'

'We'd love the company.'

They moved to a table near the back. After perusing the menu, Ally chose a burger and a milkshake. Her father decided on a steak, and Miss Kapoor picked a chicken salad. After the waitress headed off, Ally wondered if this was such a good idea. Miss Kapoor was strangely quiet, and her father seemed oddly awkward.

'Do you like teaching?' Ally asked.

'I love it,' Miss Kapoor said. 'Although I wanted to be a train driver when I was a child.'

Ally laughed. 'Really?' she said.

Miss Kapoor smiled. 'My father was a train driver,' she said. 'I didn't know there were any other jobs.'

'How long have you been teaching?' Russell asked.

'About ten years. I was at a school near Warrnambool for five years before I came here.'

'Do you miss the coast?' Russell asked.

'It's nice, but this is nice too.'

'Are you married, miss?' Ally asked.

'I'm married to my job.' Miss Kapoor angled her eyes up at Russell. 'And you?'

'Not anymore,' Russell said. 'Sharon, my wife, got cancer the year after Ally was born. She fought hard but died two years later.'

'I'm sorry to hear that.'

'Ally gets her looks and brains from her mum. Her incredibly funny sense of humour comes from me.'

Miss Kapoor smiled. 'If you say so.'

Ally spoke up. 'Miss,' she said. 'I've been thinking about the contest.'

'The contest? Oh, the ASEA contest.'

'We're certain to win as long as our third flight is successful.'

'Don't get your hopes up too high,' Miss Kapoor cautioned. 'There are entries from all over the country.'

'But we have a great entry.'

'You do, but there are hundreds of entries every year. Only one can win.'

Ally nodded, but she still thought they would win. After all, how many kids were sending balloons to the edge of space!

'The Smithsonian has a capsule from the Apollo

space program,' Ally said. 'Do you remember what it was like when man landed on the moon?'

Miss Kapoor stifled a smile. 'It was a little before my time,' she said. 'It was in 1969. I'm old, but not that old!'

They all laughed again.

Their food arrived. As they ate, Miss Kapoor told them about where she grew up and what it was like. She had been born in Jaipur, the capital of Rajasthan, in northern India. She was one of three children. Her parents had moved to Australia when she was nine. She had been back to India twice, but she didn't want to live there.

'Australia's my home now,' she said.

'I'm glad,' Russell said. 'I mean, we need teachers like you.'

Miss Kapoor asked Russell if he had any hobbies, and he told her about his painting.

'Really?' she said. 'I love art.'

This was news to Ally. 'Wow,' she said. 'Do you paint as well?'

Her teacher laughed. 'No,' she said, 'but I do have an art-related hobby.'

'What's that?' Russell asked.

'I collect thimbles,' Miss Kapoor said, looking sheepish.

Ally frowned. 'What's a thimble?' she asked.

'It's a little protective cup that you wear over your finger to help you push the needle in when you're sewing.'

'And you collect them?'

'I inherited my grandmother's sewing kit when she died. Among the things in there were three thimbles. They were quite artistic. One of them was quite old and covered in flowers. It was so pretty that I decided to find out more about them. That's when I started collecting.'

'How many do you own?' Russell asked.

'A few.'

'How many?' he persisted.

'Two hundred and twenty-one,' Miss Kapoor said, laughing. 'You probably think that's strange.'

'Not at all,' Russell said, staring at her. 'I think it's perfectly fine.'

# 22

**'WOW,' ALLY** said in the car on the way home. 'Miss Kapoor has two brothers, and she collects thimbles!'

Russell laughed. 'What's so amazing about that?' he asked.

'It just makes her seem so...human!'

'She *is* human!'

They both burst out laughing.

Driving through town, they turned onto the darkened road leading to their house. The lights of their car cut through the trees and sent shadows across the paddocks. Ally caught sight of a possum in a tree, its eyes reflecting red in the gloom. Then it was gone.

A large, black vehicle roared past them.

'They didn't have their headlights on,' Russell said. 'That's not safe.'

They were almost home now. Ahead lay an orange glow in the sky. 'That's not the sun setting,' Ally said, frowning. 'That was hours ago.'

Russell sat upright without speaking. He accelerated as they rounded the hill towards their home.

Ally's eyes widened in horror. 'The house is on fire!'

Russell skidded to a halt in front of the house. 'Stay in the car!' he said, throwing his door open. 'Don't get out!'

'But Winston—'

'I'll worry about Winston! Do NOT get out of the car!'

Shocked by the fury in his voice, she fell back in her seat as he slammed the car door and ran towards the house. Flames poured out from under the guttering and through shattered windows as Russell went crashing through the front door in search of Winston.

Ally heard something pop loudly within the building. She watched as a bright glow enveloped their kitchen and the curtains caught alight. Fire leaked from between the corrugated metal roofing while glowing embers rocketed up their chimney and into the dark sky.

With tears streaming down her face, she watched helplessly as the minutes passed, orange flames gradually engulfing their home.

*Where was Winston? Where was her father?*

The sound of sirens broke through her thoughts. Soon there were two fire engines outside their home. Firemen climbed from their vehicles, and with slow, methodical precision unfurled their hoses. One of them trained a stream of water onto the building as another aimed at spot fires that were starting to take hold in the dry grass all around the house.

Ally scrambled out of the car and was hit by the roar of the fire and the stench of dry, burnt timber.

*Where was her father?*

A police vehicle arrived. She raced over to the cops as they climbed from their car. Ally recognised one of them; he had given a presentation at her school the previous term.

'Are you all right?' he asked.

'Yes,' she said. 'But my dad went looking for our dog Winston.'

'In the house?'

Ally nodded.

The cop hurried over to a fireman. He yelled something to his companions, but Ally couldn't make out the words.

Then one of the firemen pointed. Ally followed his gaze and saw her father. He was moving a tractor away from the building. She choked back a fresh flood of tears.

*He's alive*, she thought. *He's alive.*

*But where's Winston?*

A voice cut across the crackling flames. Mrs Blunt had appeared in her nightie. She was talking to the police.

*She must have done this!* Ally thought. *She burnt down our home!*

In the next instant, Ally realised she was being ridiculous. Mrs Blunt might have been a horrible person, but she wasn't crazy. She had no reason to burn down their house.

The cop Ally had spoken to earlier pushed her back to the car as part of the roof collapsed, sending a shower of embers cascading into the sky. The spot fires doused, the firemen trained their hoses on the burning building, but it was too little, too late.

Russell appeared from the smoky gloom with something in his arms.

*No. Is that Winston? Has something happened to him?*

A policeman said something to Russell, who waved him away as Ally raced over.

'Winston!' Ally said. 'Is he...'

Russell gently placed a bundle wrapped in an old blanket into Ally's arms. A whimper came from within.

'I think his leg's broken,' Russell said. 'We've got to get him to the vet.'

It was only later, as she sat in the vet's office waiting to find out if Winston was going to be okay, that she remembered the vehicle that had driven past them in the night.

She was sure it had been a hearse.

**ALLY AWOKE** from a nightmare to find her father gently shaking her. Blinking, she found herself in a room illuminated by a harsh, fluorescent light. There were chairs, a counter, and plastic seats. Photos of birds and cats and dogs covered the walls.

*Dogs—*

'Winston—' she croaked.

'Alive,' Russell said, slumping into the seat next to her. 'His leg is broken, but it looks like he's going to be all right.'

'Did the vet say how it happened?'

'He's not sure, but it's possible that someone

kicked him.'

Ally rubbed her face. 'Who would do that?' she asked. 'Who would hurt a little dog?' Then she remembered the car without headlights. 'Drake. It was him. We passed his car on the road.'

'I think you're right,' Russell agreed wearily.

'You knew it was him?'

'I knew that was his car, but I didn't want to say anything. I rang the police while I was with the vet and told them.'

'But...why did he do it? Why did he burn our house down? And hurt Winston?'

Her father shrugged. 'Winston may have been hurt accidentally,' he said. 'And I don't know if Drake burnt the house down on purpose or not.' He rubbed his face. 'But I do know we need to get some sleep.'

'Sleep?' Ally said, confused. Their house had burnt down. Nothing remained. Where could they sleep?

'We can stay at a hotel,' Russell said. 'The owners of the Gumtree Inn rang me. They heard the house had been destroyed and said we could stay rent free for a few days.'

*Destroyed*. The word rebounded in Ally's head as

her father led her out into the darkness and to their car. *Destroyed.*

How was it possible? Everything had been so normal a few hours before. Now they'd lost everything. Photos. Books. Furniture. Her schoolbag. Their clothes. Everything ruined.

A thought suddenly occurred to her.

'No,' she said. 'No.'

She collapsed onto the gravel driveway.

'Ally?'

'The gondola. Helium tank,' she said. 'The balloon. It's all gone. Everything's gone.'

Russell knelt next to her. 'We have each other,' her father said, hugging her tightly. 'Nothing's more important than that. If I'd lost you—'

He started to cry, and Ally hugged him back.

'We're okay,' she said. 'You're right. We still have each other.'

Mr and Mrs Shaw, the owners of the Gumtree Inn, were waiting for them as they pulled into the car park. They showed them to their rooms and promised they would ring around the town to get some clothing and emergency supplies organised.

Ally staggered into the small bedroom and lay

down on the bed. She was so tired now that she almost felt faint. She closed her eyes.

*I won't be able to sleep*, she thought. *How can I sleep when...*

Her father was talking. She lifted her head and saw that daylight had arrived. Somehow the night had passed. Ally stumbled into the living room to see her dad at the front door speaking to a police officer.

'...denies any involvement,' the officer was saying. 'But your neighbour has been quite helpful.'

'Mrs Blunt?' Ally said.

The policeman peered around at Ally and introduced himself as Senior Sergeant Riley. 'She saw Drake leaving your property,' he said. 'Drake was carrying a can.'

'A can?' Russell said.

'Petrol, we think,' the policeman said.

'But why did he do it?' Ally asked. 'Why burn our house down?'

'We don't know. We can't even prove it was him at this stage, but he's assisting us with our inquiries.'

Ally nodded. That was police talk for *we think he did it*.

The policeman asked Russell to go to the station to fill out an official statement. Russell checked to make certain that Ally would be okay for an hour.

'I'm fine,' she said, looking around. There was a bowl of fruit on the table. 'I'll have something to eat.'

Ally sat in silence after Russell left. She was still in shock. She realised that she hadn't asked her father about Winston, but she knew he'd have mentioned it if he'd heard any news.

She found her bag. Her phone had been turned off. Maybe her father did that. When she turned it back on, she realised why. She had over twenty phone calls and text messages. Most were from Ping and Harmony, but a few were from Jamie and other kids in the class.

Ally started to go through them but then caught a glimpse of herself in a mirror. Her hair was everywhere. Dark shadows rimmed her eyes. She was a mess.

'I need a shower,' she muttered.

Her phone could wait.

Minutes later she emerged clean and refreshed

from the shower. She was fine with wearing the same clothes, but her hair was an issue; she didn't have a brush. She did her best to tame her unruly hair with her fingers.

There was a knock at the door. Cautiously checking through the window, she saw Mrs Shaw with a basket in her hands.

'Hello,' Ally said, opening the door.

'I'm so sorry about your house,' Mrs Shaw said. 'I've brought you some emergency supplies plus some clothing. We weren't sure about your size, so they might be a bit big.'

Ally thanked her and closed the door. Searching the bag, the first thing she found was a brush. Success! She brushed her hair into something resembling order. Checking the clothing, she found underwear, jeans and a chequered shirt that wasn't her style, but was absolutely fine under the circumstances.

Within minutes she had changed and taken another look at herself in the mirror.

*Fine*, she thought. *Now what?*

She had to start replying to people. Ally wrote a group text that she could send to everyone who had called or texted. She also posted to social media:

*Dad and I are fine and still getting ourselves together. We'll be in contact as soon as possible.*

She wondered if that was enough. She added: *Thanks for your love and best wishes.*

She had just finished when her father returned.

'Winston's fine,' were the first words out of his mouth. 'I've just spoken to the vet and he's responding well to treatment.'

'Is there any news about Drake?' Ally asked.

'The police have spoken to him,' Russell said. 'All the evidence seems to point at him.'

'Probably because he's guilty.'

'Probably.' Her father paused. 'I ran into Alan Jeffkins from the Lions Club. The town's started a collection for us.'

'A collection?'

'Money,' Russell said, his voice breaking. Ally realised he was close to tears. She hugged him. 'I told them they don't need to do that,' he said. 'I explained that the house was insured—we'll be able to rebuild once the insurance money comes through—but that will take time. Still, everyone wants to help us out.'

Ally nodded thoughtfully. The townspeople always banded together when someone suffered a disaster.

Mrs Blunt had once called Yallaroo a dirty little town, but she'd been wrong. Yallaroo was its people.

'And it looks like we'll have a place to stay,' Russell said. 'Ray Ellwood who owns the general store also has a property on Foster Street that's been empty for years. He hasn't been able to rent it to anyone, so he said we could stay there for free. I said we'll pay him a fair market rent.'

Ally vaguely remembered the place. It was an old weatherboard house with an overgrown garden, but in pretty good shape.

'Now,' Russell said, 'you need to decide what to do about your science project.'

# 24

**ALLY STARED** blankly at her father.

'The science project?' she said. 'What do you mean? We lost everything in the fire.'

'Everything?'

Ally thought about this. 'Well, we've still got the results of the first two flights,' she said. 'That was saved onto backup drives. Of course, we don't have any footage. That's why the third flight had to work. But now we've lost all our equipment.'

'So there's nothing you can do.'

There was something in the way her father spoke that made Ally stare at him. 'Everything's gone,' she said. 'We can't do another test flight. The gondola—'

'Weren't you talking about building another gondola anyway?'

Ally stopped. The last one *had* been damaged on landing. Harmony had offered to put another one together that would provide more protection for the equipment.

'Yes,' Ally said. 'But with the fire—'

'The fire's happened,' Russell said. 'Now we need to look ahead.' He reached into his bag and took out some books. 'I dropped by the library while I was out. I spoke to Samantha.'

'Samantha?'

'The librarian. There was one book in particular that she said you'd read several times.'

He showed it to Ally: *The Life of Marie Curie.*

Ally nodded. It was one of her favourites. 'Okay,' she said. 'But why—'

'It might give you some ideas. And if the people in this town are working to get us back on our feet, then we need to do the same.'

Russell said he had to go out again, and he headed off. No sooner was he gone than Ally felt she had to get out of the hotel room. She needed to take a walk.

Her father had given her a key, so she took the book with her and set off aimlessly.

Behind the hotel was Hanley Hill. You could see all the surrounding countryside from the lookout at the top. Ally clutched the book tightly as she climbed the hill. There wasn't much at the top: a car park, a few benches and a small memorial stone with a plaque acknowledging the original custodians of the land.

Ally settled down on one of the benches. She checked her phone. Three o'clock. It was later than she'd thought; somehow, she'd slept most of the day. She peered across the town. In the distance she could faintly make out the blackened smudge that was the ruins of their home.

Sighing, she opened the book.

*Marie Curie was one of the most important scientists of the twentieth century. She made contributions in...*

The sun slowly dropped in the sky, painting the clouds and dousing the dry landscape in fiery orange and red before disappearing behind the ancient hills.

As stars came out to float in the sea of night, Ally shivered. Before long it was so dark that it was almost impossible to read. She heard the crunch of footsteps on the path. Russell appeared, wordlessly handed her a jacket and a torch, and headed back towards the hotel.

Ally continued to read, a firefly in the night.

Finally, at eleven o'clock, she finished the book, and trudged back to the hotel. She found her father drinking coffee at the kitchen table.

'I finished,' was all she said as she wearily traipsed past him to her bedroom. She texted Harmony and Ping.

*R U awake?*

They replied within seconds. Ally rang them.

'Are you all right? Are you okay?' Harmony and Ping were so excited it was hard to make out who was speaking. 'How did your house burn down? Who did it?'

Ally told them everything she knew.

'Now I really am going to blow someone up!' Harmony said. 'Drake!'

'Blowing up is too good for him!' Ping said. 'We'll feed him to crocodiles! No! Attack him with spiders—'

Despite everything that had happened, Ally started to laugh.

'There's something else,' she said.

'What?' the girls replied.

'We can't give up on the science project.'

This was met with silence. 'You mean we should start a new project?' Harmony asked. 'We're building a volcano?'

'No,' Ally said. 'Proving that the Earth is round is a good project, and we're almost done. We just need to find a way to keep going.'

'But we lost everything in the fire,' Ping said.

'I know, but we can't give up,' Ally said. 'What do you know about Marie Curie?'

'Is she in year eleven?' Harmony asked.

'You idiot,' Ally said. 'She was a world-famous scientist. She was the first woman to receive a Nobel Prize, as well as the first person to receive two Nobel Prizes.

'Marie and her husband discovered two new elements—polonium and radium. They suffered all sorts of hardship to prove their discoveries: radiation poisoning, lack of sleep, working day and night for years in a dusty, cold shed.

'Then, after they had succeeded, her husband was tragically killed in an accident. It almost broke Marie, but she didn't give up.

'When World War I began, she realised that men were dying needlessly on the battlefields because doctors didn't have access to X-ray machines, so she developed vehicles that could transport mobile X-ray equipment anywhere.'

'That's amazing,' Ping said.

'Incredible,' Harmony echoed.

Ally suddenly felt like bursting into tears again but didn't know why. 'And that's why we can't stop now,' she said, swallowing hard. 'What we're facing is nothing compared to what she faced, and so many other scientists, too. Heaps of them had to suffer and struggle and fight against all sorts of difficulties—but they won in the end.'

'Okay,' Harmony said. 'What do we do?'

Ally didn't know. 'We need to replace all our equipment,' she said, slowly. 'We've already ordered a new camera, memory card and GPS. They're due to arrive at our place in the next day or two.'

'I can make another parachute,' Ping said.

'And I've got an idea about the new gondola,' Harmony added. 'It should be easy to put together.'

'Which leaves the helium bottle and balloon,' Ally said. 'The helium bottle is easy, providing the shop will rent us another one, but the balloon...'

'What about the balloon?' Harmony asked.

'I don't know,' Ally admitted. 'The balloons came from the US. They took weeks. We haven't got time to order another one before the contest ends.'

They decided to talk again in the morning, and Ally climbed into bed, exhausted. Maybe something could be done. Maybe everything wasn't lost.

*I can't give up*, she thought. *I won't!*

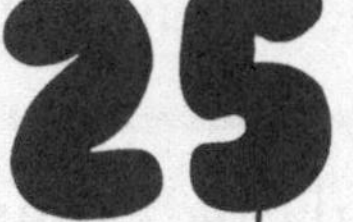

**THE NEXT** day was a flurry of activity.

Ally contacted the company in Melbourne that had supplied the helium and ordered another bottle. Her father drove her to Benalla, where they bought fabric for the parachute. They then went to Ping's house and left the fabric on her front doorstep.

What followed was difficult. They returned to their home—or what was left of it. Ally wasn't sure how she'd feel when she saw the house, but it was its absence that struck her first. Coming home had always meant rounding the hill and seeing it nestled into the landscape. It had been as much a part of the countryside as any tree or boulder.

As they drew nearer, Ally saw the little that remained: the old chimneys still stood, and the corrugated-iron roof lay about in pieces like scattered cards from some giant deck. Everything that had been made from timber—walls, doors, windows, flooring—was gone. Even the trees around the building had fallen victim to the fire, although a single old wattle at the rear had somehow survived.

Russell stopped out the front. The letterbox, path and front fence had endured too, although one side of the fence was flattened, probably pushed over by the firemen as they fought the blaze.

They climbed from the vehicle and Ally inhaled, breathing in the caustic smell of charred timber, metal and plastic. She saw that Mrs Blunt's home had been left untouched by the blaze, although some paint had peeled like sunburnt skin from the side wall.

Blue-and-white plastic police tape surrounded the rubble. Ally remembered her father had said it was still classed as a crime scene, but this made no difference to a sparrow that flitted among the wreckage.

As Ally stared at the house in silence, her eyes

focused on something burnt flapping in the yard. She let out a cry.

'Dad!' It was a piece of one of her father's paintings. 'Your paintings! They're all gone!'

Her father gave her a big hug. 'It's okay,' he soothed.

'No!' Ally said. Now she felt like the most selfish person who had ever lived. Not for one second had she thought about everything her father had lost. 'It's not okay! They were your paintings!'

'I can paint more.'

'Why did this happen?' she asked, angrily wiping away tears. 'Why?'

'I don't know,' Russell said. 'Sometimes bad things happen to good people. The main thing is that we're okay.'

The workshop at the back of the property was completely intact, as were the vehicles on the lot. Her father had been working on about half-a-dozen of them at the time of the fire.

He nodded at them. 'One of those is urgent,' he said. 'I've got to get it finished today. The rest I can finish next week.'

He disappeared into the workshop. Within minutes, Ally heard the chugging of an engine and the sound of power tools at work. She wandered around the yard, at a loose end. Their house was cordoned off, so it was impossible to pick through the ruins to see what—if anything—was still intact.

She was still wandering about aimlessly when she spotted movement at the back fence where Mrs Blunt's property joined theirs. It was the old woman, and she waved Ally over.

'I'm sorry about your house,' Mrs Blunt said. 'I heard that horrible Arthur Drake was responsible.'

Ally nodded. 'Looks that way,' she said. 'But I thought you and Mr Drake were…friends.'

Mrs Blunt sniffed. 'He wanted to buy my house,' she said. 'I told him I wasn't interested.'

'He wanted to buy ours too.'

'He was very irritating.'

Ally nodded. Mrs Blunt seemed almost *nice*.

The woman produced a jar. 'I made you some jam,' she said. 'I thought you might like it.'

'Thanks,' Ally said, surprised.

'Anyway, I'm sure the police will lay charges and he'll go to jail. It's what he deserves.'

'This must have had something to do with Hicky Saw.'

Mrs Blunt's eyes narrowed. 'What do you mean?' she asked.

Ally told her what she'd discovered at the library about Hicky Saw and his treasure.

The old woman snorted. 'Some people believe in fairy tales,' she said. 'Hicky Saw probably spent all that money on gambling and hard liquor. Arthur must have thought that burning down your home would lead him to the treasure.'

'How would that achieve anything?' Ally said.

'Who knows?' Mrs Blunt said. 'You can't understand how a crazy person thinks.' She nodded towards the workshop. 'Your father's working today?'

Ally explained he had a job to complete but would finish the remaining tractors next week. Mrs Blunt nodded thoughtfully.

'Well, good luck,' she said.

She left, and Ally took the jam back to their ute. She used her phone to search for another balloon, but the only ones she could find were too far away and would take too long to arrive.

Ally skimmed through her text messages and found one from Jamie. It read:

*Sorry about your house burning down. Harmony said in Miss Kapoor's class that she wanted to blow up Arthur Drake. miss said that was murder, and Harmony said she wanted to do it anyway.*

*Bruce and Charlotte say hi, so, 'hi'. the Tommetti triplets didn't say hi, so, no hi from them.*

*btw the website where we posted the videos and photos has had lots of hits and likes although one person said the world was flat and you're an idiot.*

*come back to school. come back come back come back.*

Ally wrote back:

*Tell the Tommetti triplets that we think lizard people burnt down our house. that'll stir them up.*

She wondered what to say about the person who had called her an idiot. She continued with:

*as far as the flat earther goes, I can't help what people think. I can only report what we discover. see you back at school.*

This done, Ally returned to the issue of trying to find a balloon for the final experiment.

**HARMONY AND** Ping gave Ally such a huge hug that she could barely speak.

'Let me go,' she gasped. 'I can't breathe!'

The girls released her. They were at Harmony's place, in her bedroom. After Russell had finished work for the day, they had returned to the hotel and found the postman had delivered the camera, GPS and memory card there. She'd brought them with her to Harmony's place so they could construct the new gondola.

'We've got a million questions,' Harmony said, 'but I've got to ask you about Winston.'

'He's okay,' Ally said. 'He's staying at the vet until we move into the place on Foster Street.'

'What's the house like?' Ping asked.

Ally hesitated. 'Not great,' she admitted. 'It'll take some cleaning to make it liveable.'

'I should send my mum over. She'd have it done in an hour.'

'I'm sure.'

'What about Drake?' Harmony asked. 'Have they arrested him yet?'

'Not yet,' Ally said. 'The police must still be searching for evidence.'

'Can't they just arrest him because he's evil?' Harmony asked.

'Unfortunately, the legal system doesn't work that way,' Ally replied.

'If I were leader, I would do away with the legal system. Anyone I thought was evil could be arrested, thrown into jail and made to eat cockroaches.'

'That sounds kind of evil in itself,' Ping pointed out.

'Hmm,' Harmony said. 'Maybe that's why they have a legal system.'

Ally asked how their preparations were going for the final flight, and Harmony pointed at some scattered gear on her bed.

'I've got everything ready for the gondola,' she said. 'We just need to put it together.'

Ally frowned. 'That looks like an esky,' she said.

'That's probably because it *is* an esky,' Harmony said. 'It's made of polystyrene, so it's really light.'

'But we do need to modify it,' Ping added.

'How do we do that?' Ally asked.

They began by painting the outside of the box. Harmony had purchased some bright orange paint. She explained that this would make it easier to find once it landed.

'We probably should have done that for the other flights,' Ally said.

It didn't take long for the paint to dry. Next, they screwed a hook into the lid, so they could attach it to the balloon with a rope, and then glued a thin layer of felt inside the box, as added protection for landing. They then taped the camera and GPS to the inside of the box, and cut a hole in the side so it could film the Earth.

Finally, they taped plastic over the hole to keep the box airtight.

'That's all we can do for now,' Harmony said.

'I'll make the parachute when I get home,' Ping said. 'The first one took a few days, but that's because I didn't know what I was doing. This one will be easy.'

'So all we need is the balloon,' Ally said, glumly. 'I've been searching online. There are plenty of places where we can buy one, but none that can deliver in time for Saturday—they're all in other countries.'

'Don't give up,' Harmony said. 'There's got to be one somewhere in Australia.'

*Sure*, Ally thought. *But where?*

When they were done, Ally called her dad and he came to pick her up. They grabbed a takeaway pizza in the town and returned to the hotel. In their absence, another basket of donations had been dropped off at their door. It contained dry goods, tinned food and toiletries. Russell went through it soberly.

'The people of this town are special,' he said, his eyes glistening. 'I don't know how we'll ever repay them.'

They ate the pizza in silence. Ally's phone rang just as she finished the last mouthful.

It was Jamie.

'Hang on,' she said to him, and told her dad she

was going for a walk.

The sun was setting as she started away from the hotel.

'How's it going?' Jamie asked. 'When will you be back?'

Ally hadn't given it much thought, but now she realised it would probably be the following Monday. They were coming up to their end-of-year exams, and she couldn't afford to miss out on any more schoolwork.

'I can send you notes from the classes you've missed,' Jamie said.

'Will I be able to read them? I've seen your handwriting.'

'Uh, maybe I'll type them.' He paused. 'By the way, did you hear the Tommetti triplets found evidence that lizard people are real?'

'*What?*'

'Someone did a DNA test proving it.'

'*You're kidding!*'

He laughed. 'Yeah,' he said. 'I'm kidding.'

'You're extremely painful,' she said. 'Has anyone ever told you that?'

'Lots of people. Anyway, we all want you back at school. Everyone's been missing you.'

'I can understand that,' she said. 'I'm a celebrity now. It's not everyone that gets their home burnt down.'

'Is it true that the new undertaker did it? And it had something to do with Hicky Saw?'

Ally filled Jamie in on what she knew. He was surprised to hear that Hicky Saw had actually been a real person.

'As real as you and me,' she said. 'But he's not haunting the streets with a saw.'

'Not even a small saw?'

'Not even a breadknife.'

Jamie said that everyone had been asking about their next balloon flight.

'Everyone's really excited about it,' he said. 'They hope it's still going ahead.'

'We're doing our best to get everything together,' Ally said. 'The big problem's the balloon. They don't sell them at the corner shop.'

They talked a bit more before signing off. Meandering back to the hotel, Ally arrived just in time to see her father hanging up the phone.

'That was the police,' he said. 'They've arrested Arthur Drake for burning down our house.'

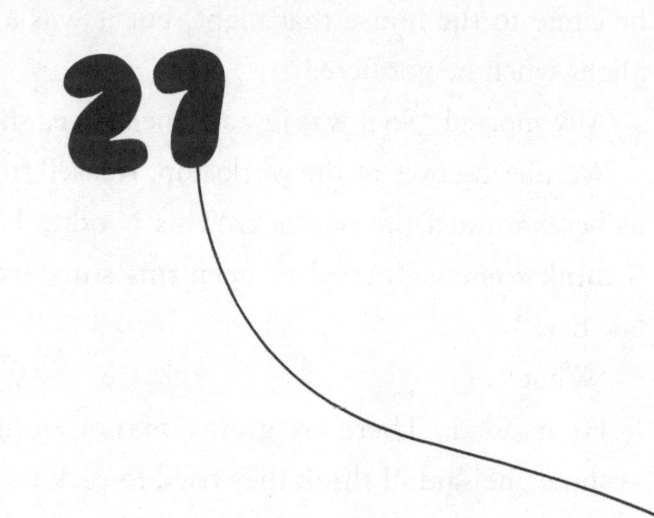

**THEY RETURNED** to their home the next morning. The police had finished their forensic work and told Russell they could search the ruins to see if anything of value could be saved.

Not too surprisingly, there wasn't anything. Everything flammable had been consumed by the fierce inferno.

'Drake sure knows how to set a fire,' Russell said. 'They must love him at barbecues.'

'He's a horrible man,' Ally said.

'He's denying any involvement,' Russell said, turning over a piece of timber with his foot. 'He said he came to the house that night, but it was already alight when he got here.'

Ally snorted. 'So it was just a coincidence,' she said.

Wandering over to the workshop, Russell frowned as he examined the padlock. 'This is odd,' he said. 'I think someone's tried to open this since we were last here.'

'What?'

He nodded. 'There are groove marks around the keyhole,' he said. 'I think they tried to pick the lock.'

Ally was speechless. After everything they'd been through, it seemed terrible that someone would try to break into her father's workshop. Russell rang the police, who promised they'd keep an eye on the property. In the meantime, he decided to take all the tools he could with them.

He spent half an hour loading the back of the ute before giving up. 'Everything else is too large to carry,' he told Ally. 'Getting the rest of the other stuff out would require a forklift, and I can't see them using one of those with Mrs Blunt so nearby.'

'I wonder if she heard anything.'

Russell went to see Mrs Blunt and returned a few minutes later.

'She says she didn't notice anything,' he said. 'But she said she sleeps pretty soundly.'

'Really? She always complained we were noisy.'

'She's not an easy woman to get on with,' Russell said, starting the car. 'Although she's making an effort to be nice.'

He stopped, as if he wanted to say more but had thought better of it.

'What is it?' Ally asked.

Russell shook his head. 'She *is* odd,' he said. 'It was nice of her to give us that jam, but she said it was homemade.'

'It's not?'

'I can tell homemade jam a mile off; my mother used to make it all the time. Mrs Blunt's jam came from a shop.'

'Why would she do that?'

'People value something that's homemade.' He shrugged. 'I suppose she wanted it to seem like she'd put in an effort.'

'She's a strange woman.'

'She is indeed.'

Arriving back at the hotel, they found the helium bottle had arrived, and Ally remembered how excited she'd been first time around. This time she felt vaguely depressed. All this effort was wasted if they couldn't track down a balloon. After they'd eaten, she sat down with her phone and continued trying to find a balloon for Saturday's test. After almost three hours of searching, she put her phone down in frustration.

'No luck?' Russell said.

'Nothing. No one in Australia sells the balloons, and one from overseas will take too long to get here.'

'Why don't you go for a walk and I'll take a look,' he offered. 'I might be old, but I know a thing or two.'

Ally nodded. She doubted her father would have any more success than her, but she needed all the help she could get. It was late Wednesday, and they were almost out of time. Heading to the Hanley Park lookout, she peered out at the dry landscape, and checked her phone again.

Harmony and Ping had sent her messages. Ping had made the new parachute in record time. She'd sent Ally and Harmony a picture of it and it looked fantastic.

They now had everything they needed—except the balloon.

A lot of people would be disappointed if she couldn't find one: Harmony and Ping, Miss Kapoor, and her father—not to mention Jamie, the kids from school and all the townspeople who'd taken an interest in the flights.

She wanted to burst into tears again.

*Marie Curie*, she thought. *What would you do?*

Ally wasn't sure. Getting the balloon wasn't something she could control. Maybe all this would end up being a complete waste.

Feeling more depressed than ever, Ally headed back to the hotel to find her father waiting.

'Do you want the good news or the bad news?' he asked.

'Uh...' Ally decided she had endured enough bad news for one week. 'Give me the good news.'

'I've found you a balloon.'

She stared at him. 'Huh?' she said.

'I've found you a balloon,' he repeated.

'You've...' Ally couldn't speak. Her father must have made a mistake. 'We can't get one from overseas. There isn't time.'

'I know.'

'Dad,' she said. 'This is a 1200-gram helium weather balloon we're talking about—'

'I know all that. That's where the bad news comes

in. There's a man in Tamworth who launches them all the time. He has a spare one he can sell us.'

'In…where?' Ally said. 'How…'

'Tamworth is about a thousand kilometres away,' Russell said, grinning. 'Feel like a road trip?'

# 28

**'THIS IS** crazy,' Ally said.

It was early Thursday morning, and Russell was reversing the ute out of the Gumtree Inn's car park. He put the vehicle into drive.

'Sometimes you have to be a little crazy to achieve your goals,' he said.

They navigated through the quiet town to the main road and followed it out of Yallaroo. High cloud smeared the horizon as they accelerated, speeding past browning fields and the distant thin crack of dark hills that divided land from sky.

There were no cars to be seen anywhere: they could

have been the only two people in the world.

Ally leaned back in her seat. The drive would take them most of the day. They would stay overnight in Tamworth and return early on Friday. If everything went according to plan, they would reach Yallaroo in time for dinner.

'And you're sure this man has the right kind of balloon?' Ally asked.

'That's what he said.'

'I just hope it's not a wasted trip.'

'If it is,' Russell said, 'it'll be a *long* wasted trip.'

The fields outside Yallaroo sparkled with early-morning sunlight as Ally and Russell sped by. A flock of white cockatoos took flight from the boughs of a dead gumtree. Cows lazily raised their heads. A crow, feeding on roadkill, hopped out of the way, returning as soon as the car had passed.

The Yallaroo road met the Hume Highway, where they accelerated again, joining the early-morning procession of cars and trucks for the first time. The highway snaked across hills and plains, cutting through patches of dry forest, and over creeks that held little or no water. These creeks would run again when rain finally came.

The highway continued north-west, skirting small towns and then the rural city of Wangaratta. The train line ran parallel to the road for a time, and a huge diesel locomotive trailed along it like a caterpillar, carrying its load to Sydney. Then the road peeled away, and they continued onwards through open countryside.

'Australia's a big country,' Ally said.

Russell nodded. 'It's not small.'

The hours passed. They reached the city of Wodonga, on the Victorian side of the border, before crossing the Murray River to its sister city—Albury—on the other side.

'Welcome to New South Wales,' Russell said.

'Funny,' Ally said. 'Feels just like Victoria.'

Russell shook his head. 'They play a strange type of football on this side,' he said, grinning. 'Other than that, they're okay.'

They drove on. The road held few surprises. There were hills. Clumps of trees. Kangaroos, possums and other unidentifiable roadkill, the stench of which sometimes clutched at the backs of their throats.

Ally took out her phone and followed their signal on the map as the kilometres passed. They still had a long way to go.

Her father turned off the highway so they could drive through Holbrook.

'Why are we coming this way?' Ally asked.

'Just to be tourists for a moment.'

They passed a black cylindrical shape half buried in a park adjacent to the road.

'Holbrook was named after a naval officer,' Russell explained. 'They have a submarine here—HMAS Otway—to honour him.'

Climbing from the car, Russell took a photo of them in front of the submarine as a souvenir.

They continued on.

Just over an hour later they reached Gundagai, and another opportunity for a photo.

'It's the famous *Dog on the Tuckerbox*,' Russell said as they stopped at a statue near the town. It was a bronze dog sitting on a box. 'It's based on a poem. Tuckerboxes were a type of lunchbox. Apparently, the dog chose to...er, do its business on the tuckerbox.'

'And they wrote a poem about it?'

'Bullock drivers used to write a lot of poetry and stories while they travelled. It was a way to fill in the time.'

They took a picture, found a roadside café, and stopped for snacks for the road before driving on. The towns rolled by: Young, Cowra, Molong. At least the road was now taking them through towns rather than skirting them; it made for a more interesting drive.

A lot of places had names bigger than the towns. These places had no shops, a couple of houses, and nothing more. Ally wondered how the people lived out here. It was like being marooned on a desert island.

She closed her eyes. When she awoke, she saw great herds of black cows in paddocks, and a wave of galahs breaking across the sky.

'Did I sleep for long?' she asked.

'Yes. You were drooling.'

Ally glanced at her phone. It was almost three o'clock. She'd been asleep for ages.

'Great.' She wiped her mouth. 'It looks a little greener here.'

'Still dry, though,' Russell said. 'And summer's barely started.'

'Where are we?'

They drove through a larger town.

'Dunedoo,' her father said.

He pronounced it done-ee-doo.

'That's a strange name,' Ally said.

'A pretty town, though.'

They stopped and climbed out, and Ally felt the full brunt of the heat. It was easy to forget how hot it was outside when you were locked within the air-conditioned comfort of the ute. They bought some cold drinks, clambered back in and took to the road again.

More towns skirted past as the afternoon slid on. At least now Ally was starting to feel some anticipation. With every kilometre that passed, they were another kilometre closer to the balloon—if it existed.

'What's his name?' she asked.

'Whose name?'

'The man with the balloon.'

'Rod McCarrick.'

Ally repeated the name and it rolled off her tongue.

Road signs started appearing with the name Tamworth on them.

'We're almost there,' Ally said.

'Almost.'

The word had a different meaning on a drive this long. It was almost dinnertime before they reached the outskirts of Tamworth. It was a regional city, made famous by its annual country music festival. Russell turned onto a side road, and then another side road. They weaved through suburbs that could have been any streets anywhere in Australia.

Slowing the ute, Russell started reading out the house numbers. 'Six, eight, ten,' he read.

'Twelve,' Ally said, her voice rising. 'Fourteen, sixteen, eighteen.'

Russell stopped the car. 'Twenty,' he said.

They looked out at a single-storey brick house that had a rose garden out the front.

'We're here,' Ally said.

# 29

**ROD MCCARRICK** was a lanky, sun-tanned man with grey hair, some missing teeth and a lopsided smile. 'So you're our balloonist!' he said, beaming at Ally. 'Come on in!'

They followed him into a tidy living room.

'Wow,' Ally said.

She peered about in amazement. The walls were covered in photos of stars and planets. There was a globe of the Earth on a pedestal in the corner. A bookcase was crammed full of books about astronomy and the planets.

'Did you take these?' Russell asked, pointing to

the photos.

Rod nodded. 'I did,' he said. 'I have a lot of hobbies. Astrophotography is one of them.'

Ally's eyes swept the room, finally coming to rest on a small, rectangular parcel on a seat.

'You've got eyes like a hawk,' Rod said.

Ally smiled. 'That's the balloon.'

'It's got a maximum burst altitude of thirty-seven kilometres, but that depends on the weight of your payload.'

Ally paid him for the balloon, and he asked her why she needed it.

'It's for a contest,' Ally said. 'The first prize is a trip to the Smithsonian.'

'I've been there! You'll love it. What does the contest involve?'

'We have to use the scientific method to prove something. We're proving that the world is round.'

Rod burst out laughing. 'Strange that some people think it's flat!' he said. 'But some people will believe anything.'

'There's so much junk on the internet,' Russell said. 'We've left the information age behind for the *mis*-information age.'

'Have you been filming your efforts?' Rod asked Ally.

'We've got some footage, but none of the actual flights,' she said, telling him about the problems they'd encountered. 'We hope to have more luck this time.'

He gave her some advice about making certain there was sufficient padding for the equipment, and how to mount the camera. Ally thanked him as they headed out to their car.

'I wish you success in your efforts,' Rod said.

'Thanks,' Ally said, as they started away.

Rod waved. 'Aim for the stars!'

'Thanks!'

They drove through town. Russell had already rented a hotel for the night. After dropping off their gear, they had dinner at a restaurant before turning in early.

The alarm the next morning awakened Ally from a deep sleep. It was hard to believe they had to do the return journey.

'At least tonight we'll be sleeping at home,' Russell said, rubbing his neck. 'That bed was *very* uncomfortable.'

They hit the road. Ally was sorry that they couldn't

stay in Tamworth, but she was also excited.

*We've got a balloon*, she thought. *We can launch tomorrow.*

Soon the towns were whipping by. Russell drove on all through the long day, stopping for short breaks as they went. As they reached the border just after four o'clock, Ally felt a kind of elation come over her.

'We're getting closer,' she said.

'Counting off the kilometres?'

'Absolutely.'

'Me too. This is a lot of driving.'

There were no short cuts they could take to get home any faster. They kept on, kilometre after kilometre, stopping only once more for petrol. Finally, as evening approached, they reached the turn-off for Yallaroo, and pulled into the hotel car park. Russell shut off the engine and they looked at each other.

'Did we really just drive to Tamworth and back?' Russell asked.

'Yep,' Ally said, glancing at the balloon in the back seat. 'We sure did.'

After they'd lugged their gear inside, Ally got on the phone to Harmony and Ping.

'I've got the balloon,' she said.

'I can bring over the parachute,' Ping said.

'And I can bring the gondola,' Harmony said.

'That's great,' Ally said, yawning. 'But make it soon. Dad and I are both exhausted.'

It was just before seven o'clock when the girls arrived, but Ally was already almost asleep. Ping attached the parachute. She hadn't brought her laptop, but she would bring it the next morning. Russell cast an approving eye over their construction as he sipped a cup of coffee.

'That looks good,' he said. 'Very neat.'

Examining the lid of the esky, Ally saw that Harmony had installed an additional bracket. 'What's that for?' she asked.

'Oh,' Harmony said, innocently. 'You'll see.'

As much as Ally cajoled her, Harmony refused to explain the bracket's purpose.

'I think a lot of people will be at tomorrow's launch,' Ping said. 'The word's got around.'

'Great,' Ally said. The launch was due to take place at eight o'clock the next morning. She wondered if they'd forgotten anything, but she couldn't think anymore. Her brain had turned to mush. 'I'll see you at the Mitchells' farm.'

She ushered them out. It wasn't long before she had changed into her pyjamas and was climbing into bed.

'Dad,' she said.

'Yep?'

'Thanks for everything.'

'That's okay,' he said, turning out the light. 'That's what dads are for.'

Ally wondered if she'd actually be able to sleep, but she drifted off immediately and found herself standing among the ruins of their house. Mist filled the air. It swirled around her like ghostly streamers. A figure was walking between the rusting pieces of farm equipment. It turned and slowly started towards her.

*Hicky Saw!*

She recognised him from his picture in the newspaper. Ally should have felt terrified, but instead felt sad. 'You're not a monster,' she said. 'You're just a person.'

'I need help,' Hicky Saw said. His mouth didn't move, but Ally could still hear his words. 'I need things to be made right.'

'How can I do that?'

Before he could reply, the mist swirled around and swallowed him whole. Rain started to fall. Ally turned her face to the sky and watched it tumbling down.

When she looked down next, she saw a flash of green at her feet.

A eucalyptus tree had started to grow amid the ruins. It was only small, but it was a bright, fresh healthy green sapling.

'Wow,' she said. 'That's really beautiful.'

A voice wafted through the fog.

'...can't understand how a crazy person thinks...'

'Mrs Blunt?' Ally peered around. 'Is that you?'

'...making an effort to be nice...'

'Dad?'

Ally frowned. Something was wrong, but she wasn't sure what. It had to do with Hicky Saw—

*Brrrrrrrr!*

The alarm clock jolted Ally from her sleep.

# 30

**THEY HAD** the car packed in minutes. Russell made Ally check twice to make certain she had everything.

'Gondola,' she said. 'Complete with camera, memory card and GPS.'

'Check,' Russell said.

'Parachute.'

'Check.'

'Helium bottle.'

'Check.'

'Balloon.'

'Check.'

She rubbed her chin. 'And Ping is bringing the laptop,' she said. 'That's everything.'

'Then let's get this show on the road.'

They drove through town. It wasn't until they reached the Mitchells' farm that they saw the field opposite was already filled with vehicles. People were everywhere. Senior Sergeant Riley was directing traffic. He waved Russell over.

'Next time you're holding a public event,' Riley said, raising an eyebrow, 'let us know in advance.'

'Huh?' Russell said.

'These people are all here to see the balloon take off.'

'*Really?*' Ally said.

'There's still some parking available,' the police officer said. 'Someone saved you a spot.'

He pointed to Miss Kapoor, who was waving frantically at them. They hurried over to her.

'I thought you'd never get here,' she said, giving Ally a quick hug.

'This is...' Ally peered around in astonishment. 'Amazing.'

Harmony and Ping rushed over.

'Everyone's here!' Ping gushed. 'It's bigger than

the Olympics! Well, maybe not as big, but it's bigger than—'

'Let's get set up,' Harmony interrupted.

Russell, Miss Kapoor, Joe Mitchell and Jamie's mum, Laura, cordoned off an area to keep the crowds back. Ally kept glancing around as they got out their gear. It really did seem like half the town had turned up. A lot of schoolkids were there. Even the Tommetti triplets.

A few people approached Russell with commiserations about their lost home. He thanked everyone for their good wishes.

Harmony produced something from her backpack.

Ally stared. 'What is that?' she asked.

Harmony shrugged. 'You said you wanted Barbie,' she said, innocently.

Ally and Ping burst out laughing. Harmony had dressed the Barbie doll in closefitting imitation black leather pants and a lacy blood-red top. She had dyed black hair and wore black eye make-up and lipstick. Tiny tattoos adorned her arms. A silver piercing decorated one eye.

'It's fan-girl Barbie,' Harmony said. 'She loves Blood Guzzling Unicorns as much as me.'

They attached Barbie to the bracket and checked the camera. The memory card had several hours of recording time. Ping consulted the laptop as they turned on the GPS.

'It's connected,' she said. 'I'm getting a clear signal.'

'Now let's see to the balloon,' Ally said.

Russell, Miss Kapoor and Joe Mitchell helped to keep the balloon steady as the girls inflated it with helium. Unlike last time, the morning was still with only a few clouds in the sky. It was a perfect day to fly a balloon.

A hush fell over the crowd as the balloon got bigger and bigger. Soon it was bigger than a person. Harmony tied it off and connected it to the rope.

'Is everything still working?' Ally asked as the balloon struggled to fly free.

Harmony and Ping checked the laptop one last time.

'Everything's fine,' Ping said. 'The temperature is fourteen point six degrees Celsius. The wind is coming from the south-south-west at four knots.'

'Okay,' Ally said. 'It's time.'

*This is our last chance*, she thought. *It's over if it doesn't work this time.*

The girls allowed the balloon to rise until they were only gripping the gondola.

'Should we say something important?' Ping asked.

Ally thought. 'Fly as high as you can,' she said.

They let go.

The balloon soared straight up into the sky. The townspeople burst into applause, and then cheers, as the balloon rocketed up. Ally couldn't speak. Her mouth hung open as she watched the balloon zoom away.

*It's going to the edge of space*, she thought.

'Come on,' Harmony said. 'We need to get moving.'

People started piling into their cars. Russell climbed into the front seat of the ute as the girls climbed into the back and huddled around the laptop.

'It's already at one kilometre and rising steadily,' Ping said.

Ally peered through the window. She could still see the balloon, but it was already a tiny dot in the sky.

'Let's go,' she said.

Cars had begun to leave the paddock and were clogging the road. It looked like some people were going off to get on with their day, but others were keen to join the pursuit. Fortunately, Senior Sergeant

Riley was able to maintain order long enough to allow Russell through.

'Good luck!' he yelled.

They sped up the road.

'Its height is two and half kilometres,' Ping said. 'Drifting north-west at four knots.'

'So far so good,' Harmony said.

Russell guided them north along Dookie Road, passing fields that were flat and sparsely dotted with eucalypts. Rounding a hill, Ally saw the remains of a burnt paddock.

*Must have been a bushfire through here*, she thought.

The blackened trees reminded Ally of her dream. She couldn't remember all the details, but Hicky Saw had been in it, as well as Mrs Blunt. There had been something disturbing about the dream. Something she needed to remember.

*What was it?*

They continued onwards for more than another hour before the balloon finally burst and released the gondola. It only took another hour for them to find it. The gondola had landed near a side road at Mount Manor. There were still more than a dozen vehicles following behind them when they found it.

Everyone piled from their cars to watch the girls. Barbie had been thrown from the gondola on impact but lay only a short distance away. Ally carefully eased the lid off the esky. The camera and contents were all intact.

'Everything seems fine,' she said.

# 31

**THEY WENT** to Harmony's house to watch the footage. The first time, they watched in dumb amazement. The second time, they squealed a lot. The third time, they whooped.

Ally doubted she would ever tire of seeing it. The curvature of the planet was obvious; the Earth was round.

'Wow,' she said, breathlessly. 'We did it.'

'We did,' Ping agreed.

'We sure did,' Harmony said. 'Now we just need to write up the results.'

'And win the contest,' Ally said.

'That too,' Ping said.

It took them the rest of the day, but by evening they'd copied the video onto Ping's laptop, recorded their results and typed up their final report. They also sent a copy of the video to Jamie so he could upload it to his website.

Russell picked Ally up after dinner.

'Everything finished?' he asked as she climbed into the ute.

'We're sending the report first thing Monday morning,' she said. 'The closing date is Wednesday, so we'll send it express post.'

'You've done a great job,' he said.

'We're going to win the contest,' Ally said. 'No one else will have produced anything like this.'

'Maybe not,' Russell said. 'But don't get too hung up about the contest. There will be a lot of entries, and you don't know what other people are submitting.'

Ally's phone pinged.

'Wow,' she said, her eyes widening. 'Jamie said the Twilight Movie people want to show our footage before the next film!'

'The whole town's excited,' Russell said. 'We haven't had anything this big happen since...well...ever!'

They drove through town towards the hotel. It was early evening now, and the streetlights had come on. A car came towards them with its headlights off. Russell flashed his lights, and the other driver snapped theirs on.

'That's like Drake's car,' Ally said, 'the night our house burnt down.'

A sense of disquiet stirred in her belly.

'We were lucky we spotted him,' Russell said.

Ally nodded, silent.

Russell glanced over at her. 'What is it?' he asked. 'Are you okay?'

'Dad,' she said, 'we saw him just before we reached the house.'

'That's right.'

'But the house was already fully alight.'

'That *is* odd,' Russell admitted. 'Maybe he waited for the fire to take hold before he drove off.'

'What reason did Drake give for being near our place?'

'He told the police he was visiting Mrs Blunt.'

Ally considered this. 'They were dating,' she said, 'but later Mrs Blunt called him a crazy person.'

'She never has anything good to say about anyone.'

'But she's been friendly to us ever since the fire,' Ally said. 'And who rang the fire brigade?'

'Mrs Blunt.'

'She could have waited until the house was well alight before ringing them.'

Russell slowed the car and pulled over. 'What are you saying?' he asked.

'What if Drake didn't burn our house down? What if Mrs Blunt did?'

'But why?'

'For Hicky Saw's treasure.'

'There isn't any treasure.'

'Maybe not, but they think there is.' Her mind was racing now. 'Mrs Blunt wanted us out of the way so she could find the treasure.'

'By burning down our house? That doesn't make any sense.'

'I can't explain that,' Ally admitted. 'But what if Mrs Blunt wanted all the treasure for herself? Why share it with Drake when she didn't have to?'

Russell rubbed his chin. 'Drake told the police the house was already on fire when he got there,' he said. 'Maybe it was.'

'I bet Mrs Blunt invited him around so he'd be at

the scene of the crime.

'It all sounds pretty thin,' he said. 'Although...'

Ally waited.

'That jam struck me as strange,' he said. 'And she was really curious as to when I'd be back working.'

'She asked me the same question. She wanted us out of the way so she could search for the treasure.'

Russell started the car again and headed not for the hotel but for their home. It was almost completely dark when they pulled into their driveway.

There were no lights anywhere. Russell produced a torch from the glove compartment. It cut through the darkness as they made their way past the burnt remains of their house.

'I don't believe there's any buried treasure,' he said. 'There's no way—'

'*Ooooooohhhhh...*'

A plaintive cry drifted across the graveyard of rusted farm machinery.

'What was that?' Russell said.

Ally swallowed. 'Hicky Saw?' she asked.

'I don't think so.'

The cry came again.

'That came from the workshop,' Russell said.

They approached the old building. Someone had broken off the lock, and the front door was wide open. They edged in cautiously and shone the torch around. Shadows danced across the walls.

'Dad!' Ally cried, grabbing his arm. 'There.'

A dark shape lay in the corner.

'What is that?' Russell asked.

The old carpet covering the floor had been pulled back, revealing a trapdoor and a steep set of timber steps.

A figure at the bottom gave a ghostly moan.

'*Ooooooohhhhh...*'

Ally stifled a scream as Russell shone the light down the steps.

'Mrs Blunt?' Ally said.

The old woman lay in a heap at the bottom. She groaned again but did not move. Russell and Ally carefully descended.

'She's fallen down the stairs,' Russell said, quickly examining the woman. 'She needs an ambulance.'

'What is this place?' Ally asked, peering around the gloom.

'An old fruit cellar, I think,' Russell said. He

checked his phone. 'I've got no reception. You stay with her. I'll go for help.'

Handing her the torch, he climbed out. Ally heard his footsteps recede into the distance.

'Mrs Blunt,' Ally said, 'we're getting you help.'

The old woman groaned. 'The treasure,' she muttered. 'Hicky Saw...'

She lost consciousness. Ally shone the torch around the cellar, showing walls lined with dusty shelves. In the middle of the room sat a single timber table with a few empty jars and a cobwebbed glass on it. A bundle of rags lay in the corner.

Ally focused the light on the rags.

*What are they?*

It took her a moment to realise. Drawing in a sharp breath, she almost screamed again, but then reminded herself.

*Ghosts aren't real.*

Summoning up all her courage, she swallowed hard before nodding to the motionless figure.

'Hello, Hicky,' she said. 'I'm Ally.'

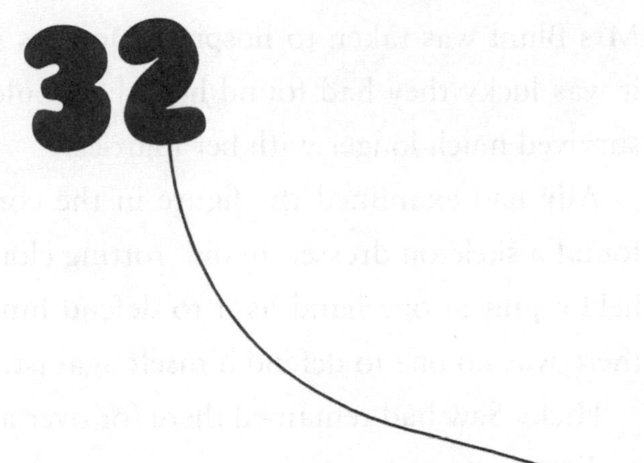


**'SO IT** was Hicky Saw's ghost,' Ben Tommetti said.

'Or was he a zombie?' Bill Tommetti asked.

'Or a lizard person?' Bob Tommetti said. 'He was a lizard person, wasn't he?'

'He wasn't any of those things,' Ally said. 'But it *was* Hicky Saw.'

They were sitting in the science room waiting for Miss Kapoor to arrive. Weeks had passed since Ally and her father had made their discoveries in the underground cellar. She had already explained the events of that night several times, but people loved to hear it all again.

Both the police and an ambulance had arrived, and Mrs Blunt was taken to hospital. Doctors said later it was lucky they had found her; she wouldn't have survived much longer with her injuries.

Ally had examined the figure in the corner, and found a skeleton dressed in old, rotting clothing. He held a gun in one hand as if to defend himself, but there was no one to defend himself against.

Hicky Saw had remained there for over a century, undisturbed until now.

'He'd helped to build both houses and knew about the cellar,' Ally explained. 'After that last shootout with police, he must have tried hiding in there but fallen down the stairs. The police found a big crack in his skull.'

She shuddered when she thought about him dying alone in the darkness. His body had been there all those years while she was growing up. She had played in her father's workshop hundreds of times, not suspecting that Hicky Saw lay just beneath her feet.

'Mrs Blunt confessed to burning down our house,' Ally continued. 'Drake had been pretending he was interested in dating her, but he was too curious about the history of the houses, and she realised he was after

Hicky Saw's treasure. She knew both houses had been built at the same time, but the difference was that our property had the underground fruit cellar.

'Mrs Blunt knew the treasure wasn't in her house, and she doubted it was in ours. If it were there, we'd have found it already. She guessed—quite correctly—that Hicky had used the cellar as a hiding place.

'There was no way she could get to it with us on the property, so she burned our house down to get us out of the way and find the treasure.'

Except there was no treasure. Once there may have been, but all the police had found on his body were some betting stubs. He had likely gambled—and lost—all his money at the races.

Next to him lay a letter he planned to post to his mother. Ally thought again about the letter. Stamped and ready to post, it was a heartfelt note, saying how much he regretted becoming a criminal and that he looked forward to one day returning home.

This last part, at least, was finally coming true. Hicky Saw was to be buried next to his mother.

Ally sat back. The last two weeks had been busy. They'd sat their final exams and handed in the last of their assignments. With Christmas fast approaching,

Ally had bought Christmas cards and gifts. They'd also moved into the place on Foster Street, where they would live until their new home was built.

Miss Kapoor entered the room looking excited.

'Children!' she said. 'I have news! Wonderful news!'

Everyone glanced at each other.

*What's this about?* Ally wondered. *What could—*

Her eyes opened wide.

*The contest!*

Barely able to contain herself, Ally forced herself to sit still as Miss Kapoor continued.

'Congratulations to everyone who entered the ASEA contest,' she said. 'Everyone's entries were most impressive! Most impressive!'

*Get on with it!*

'Of course, there can be only one winning team and that team is here at Yallaroo! I have great pleasure in announcing that the winners of the Australian Scientific Education Association contest are...'

*Yes!* Ally thought. *It's us!*

'The Busy Bees!'

Jamie yelled out in amazement. Charlotte squealed. Bruce fell out of his chair. The Tommetti triplets groaned. Harmony and Ping clapped.

Ally felt sick.

*The...Busy Bees?*

Harmony reached over and gave her arm a sympathetic squeeze.

*I'm sorry*, she mouthed.

Miss Kapoor was still talking.

'...an amazing job in identifying the types of flowers that are most helpful for bees to survive,' Miss Kapoor said. 'The judging team said it was one of the most important projects that had ever been submitted. It will help the scientific community...'

But Ally had tuned her out. *We didn't win. We didn't win.* The words kept echoing in her mind. *We didn't win.*

She couldn't focus for the rest of the lesson.

At the final bell, she climbed from her chair and made her way to the door where she bumped into Jamie.

'Hey,' she said, trying to smile. 'Congratulations...'

'Thanks.' He looked embarrassed. 'I didn't expect it.'

'Bees are important,' she said.

'I wish you'd won,' Jamie said. 'Your project—'

Ally cut him off. 'It's fine,' she said.

Charlotte appeared at his side. 'Isn't it great?' she said. 'We're going to the Smithsonian!'

'Yeah,' Ally said. 'That's great.'

She turned, walked out and went to the girls' toilets. Closing the cubicle door, she sat down and promptly burst into tears. Five minutes later she heard a tapping.

'Ally?' Harmony's voice came through the wood. 'Are you alive in there?'

'I'm fine,' she said, wiping away tears.

'Are you sure?' Ping said. 'I thought maybe you'd had a stroke...or a heart attack...or something...'

Ally opened the door and looked into her friends' worried faces. She wasn't sure if she wanted to yell or burst into tears again, so instead she pulled them both close.

'Group hug,' she said.

# 33

**'ARE YOU** ready?' Russell called.

'Almost,' Ally said.

It was Friday. School had ended for the year and their film of the final balloon flight was being shown at the Twilight Movie festival. Harmony had trimmed the whole flight down to fifteen minutes and added a soundtrack.

'We don't want to be late,' Russell continued from the other room. 'We're picking someone up on the way.'

'Who?' Ally asked.

'Danika.'

Ally frowned. 'Who's Danika?' she asked.

'Oh.' There was silence. 'Miss Kapoor.'

Ally sauntered into her father's room. Gone were his overalls. He was neatly dressed in a nice checked shirt, clean jeans and black shoes.

'It's Danika now, is it?' Ally asked.

Russell rolled his eyes. 'Don't be silly,' he said. 'She just wanted a lift.'

'Sure,' Ally said. 'Whatever.'

Her eyes settled on a set of paints and a blank canvas in the corner.

'You bought new paints?' she said.

'Time to start again.'

'More houses and trees?'

'I think I've mastered houses and trees,' Russell said. 'It's time I moved onto mountains and lakes.'

'Good on you. The world needs artists as well as scientists.'

Ally's phone beeped to say she had a new email. She frowned at the sender's name: Cheryl Maguire.

*Who on Earth is Cheryl Maguire?* she wondered.

She read:

*Dear Ally,*

*My colleagues and I found your website online and are most impressed by your efforts to prove that the Earth is round.*

*We would like...*

Ally's eyes widened as she read the email. Then she checked it again to make certain she had read it right.

'Ally?' Russell said. 'Is everything okay?'

'I just got an email from one of the scientists at the Parkes Observatory in New South Wales,' she said. 'It's the radio observatory they used to relay the signal when man first landed on the moon. The scientists saw our videos online and were really impressed. They've invited me, Harmony and Ping to come and visit!'

'That's wonderful!' Russell said. 'Congratulations!'

Ally realised she was beaming. Not only would they have a chance to examine the radio telescope, but they'd also be given a special VIP tour of the facility.

'They say we've helped to set an example for young people everywhere,' Ally said, starry-eyed. 'It's not every day you get to do that.'

Her father gave her a huge hug. 'You are fantastic,' he said.

'Thanks, Dad,' she said. 'I love you.'

'I love you too.' He glanced at his watch. 'We'd better get moving. Don't want to be late. We've got your movie as well as the main feature.'

They were showing the 1950s version of *The Day the Earth Stood Still.* It was one of Ally's favourite old films.

They drove through town, picked up Miss Kapoor along the way and continued to the festival. Ally met up with Ping and Harmony and gave them the good news.

They squealed with delight.

'That's amazing,' Ping said.

Harmony checked her phone. 'This is incredible,' she said. 'Parkes is one of the radio observatories involved in the Breakthrough Listen program. That's where they search for signals from alien civilisations.'

'We can do a road trip on the way,' Ping said. 'Maybe go to Canberra, and then Sydney and maybe even—'

Before she could continue, the man who programmed the films got up to speak.

'Tonight we have a special feature before our main movie,' he said. 'Three of our own Yallaroo girls put together a science project that inspired the whole town. Now we can see the results of all their hard work.'

The screening began with some footage of Jamie's, showing the girls assembling the balloon on the ground. The next shot came from the camera mounted on the balloon, as it was released into the sky. It tilted downwards momentarily, catching a glimpse of Ally, Harmony and Ping.

'That's us,' Ping said.

She said that every time.

'I know,' Harmony said.

She said that every time too.

The camera lifted higher, showing fields and roads around Yallaroo before soaring skyward. It rushed through clouds as if drawn upwards by an invisible string.

The landscape spread out below like a huge map. All the fields merged together. Yallaroo was reduced to a smudge. A silver and grey shape appeared in the distance.

'That's Melbourne,' Ally heard someone say.

She glanced around at the crowd. Many of these people would have seen the video on the internet, but they were still spellbound. The balloon kept rising, breaking through more clouds. The coast of Victoria swung into view.

Tilting upwards, the camera caught a glimpse of the sky above, no longer blue but black. The balloon had travelled beyond the breathable atmosphere. The camera spun around and was briefly blinded by the harsh sun.

Then, angling downwards, the camera pointed directly at the curving horizon.

'Look at that!' a voice said in amazement. 'The world *is* round!'

Ally glanced about. It was Ben Tommetti who had spoken. A titter of laughter came from the crowd.

The balloon kept rising until it finally seemed to hover, peering quietly across a mottled marble of blue and white. Spanning the horizon lay the thin layers of the atmosphere, bands of colour that morphed from pale turquoise to azure blue, and finally to deep black. Within that darkness lay the great silence of the universe.

For what seemed an eternity, the balloon dangled above the planet, caught between the Earth and space—until suddenly the camera jerked, lurching about, and they saw hundreds of pieces of broken latex. The balloon had burst.

The camera swung up, down and around as the

gondola fell, its descent slowed by the parachute. The world came back into sharp focus.

*It's a big planet*, Ally thought.

Soon fields and farms were visible. A forest came into view. A road. A fence line. The field grew near, bounced and fell sideways. The gondola had landed.

The audience burst into applause, whooping and cheering.

'Stand up,' Russell urged.

Ally, Harmony and Ping stood up uncertainly, and the crowd applauded even louder.

Ally remembered something that Mrs Blunt had said. What was it?

*No one in this dirty little town has ever achieved anything.*

Ally couldn't stop herself smiling.

*We proved her wrong*, she thought.

Before the main feature was due to start, Jamie came over and sat next to her. He didn't speak for a while, but then he leaned closer.

'I'm sorry about the contest,' he said. 'I know that you really wanted to win.'

'It's okay,' Ally said. 'I'm happy for you. Anyway, I've got some good news.'

She told him about the invitation to Parkes Observatory.

'That's fantastic,' he said. 'Still, we're going to miss you while we're away.'

Russell sidled over. 'Actually,' he said, 'I have some news about that.'

'What is it?' Ally asked.

Her father rubbed his chin thoughtfully. 'It's about Hicky Saw,' he said. 'Hicky didn't have any living family. His only surviving relative was his mother, and she's long gone. It seems we inherit all his worldly possessions.'

'Uh,' Ally said. 'Like…what?'

'Well, there isn't a lot,' Russell admitted. 'Just his clothing and what he had with him.'

'The only thing he had was his gun.'

'And the letter.'

'Yep,' Ally agreed. 'And the letter.'

'The gun's an important historical piece, as is the letter. We'll be donating them both to a museum for everyone to see.' Russell paused. 'But it's the envelope that's special, or rather, the stamp.'

'The stamp?'

'It's a rare Kangaroo and Map stamp,' Russell said.

'There's only a handful in existence, so it's worth around twenty thousand dollars.'

Ally's mouth fell open. 'You're kidding,' she said.

'I'm not,' Russell said. 'Hicky Saw really did have a treasure, but he didn't know it.'

Ally pointed at Harmony and Ping. 'If we're going to the Smithsonian…' she started.

'Ping and Harmony can come too,' Russell said. 'As long as it's okay with their parents.'

The girls screamed with excitement and would have kept on screaming except the main feature was starting. As Ally sat there watching the opening credits, she thought she had never been happier in her whole life.

When the movie finished, Ally wanted to hang around and talk, but then a drop of water landed on her head. And another. And another. It started as a shower but soon turned into a downpour.

Laughing, people started running to their cars as the heavens opened up, and rain pounded the town. Ally yelled out to Ping and Harmony that she would see them at Moo Moo's the next day. She told Jamie she would see him during the holidays.

Ally, her father and Miss Kapoor piled into the ute as rain bucketed down over the dry countryside.

'This is long overdue,' Russell said as he eased their car into the line of traffic.

'And we need more of it,' Miss Kapoor said.

'A lot more,' Ally agreed.

Miss Kapoor smiled at Ally. 'It's so exciting that you're going to Parkes. I read an article recently that said Parkes has been used to track spacecraft travelling to Mars.'

'Wow,' Ally said, thinking. 'Mars.'

'No one's been there yet,' Russell said.

'Really?' Ally said.

*Wow*, she thought. *Maybe I'll go there one day.*

They drove on through the pouring rain.